Lincolnshire

KT-140-719

COMMUNITIES, CULTURAL SERVICES
and ADULT EDUCATION

**This book should be returned on or before
the last date shown below.**

To renew or order library books please telephone 01522 782010
or visit www.lincolnshire.gov.uk
You will require a Personal Identification Number.
Ask any member of staff for this.

EC. 199 (LIBS): RS/L5/19

THE EXPEDITER .

Johnny Doyle had spent all his life in the East and only the death of his brother forced him to journey to the strange land of the West — a place, he was soon to find, where trouble could shoot out unexpectedly from any quarter. To cope, he had to learn the ways of the West. However, once he was taught to ride, he could take to the vengeance trail. There were hard men out there, but when it came to the showdown, would any be as tough as Johnny Doyle? Not for nothing was he known as the Expediter.

JACK DARBY

THE EXPEDITER

Complete and Unabridged

LINFORD
Leicester

First published in Great Britain in 2004 by
Robert Hale Limited
London

First Linford Edition
published 2005
by arrangement with
Robert Hale Limited
London

British Library CIP Data

Darby, Jack
    The expediter.—Large print ed.—
Linford western library
1. Western stories
2. Large type books
I. Title
823.9′2 [F]

ISBN 1–84617–013–3

Published by
F. A. Thorpe (Publishing)
Anstey, Leicestershire

Set by Words & Graphics Ltd.
Anstey, Leicestershire
Printed and bound in Great Britain by
T. J. International Ltd., Padstow, Cornwall

This book is printed on acid-free paper

*To Adam — one-time reader who
is now an author in his own
'Wright' — in thanks for his interest*

1

Three men strode along the sidewalk. In an unbending phalanx they pushed aside anyone who didn't step smartly out of their way. Well-dressed, they looked out of place amongst the poor inhabitants of the area.

The stench and the heat of the streets were stifling. Fumes reeked from the open sewers. The men crossed the drag and paused before a huge pile of building. The block was divided into a host of tenements, tenanted mainly by women plying the same trade.

They entered and mounted the stairs, brushing past a fellow in shirt-sleeves seated on the stair. Coming to the first room one of the men, elaborately moustachioed, tried the knob. When it refused to give he turned and nodded to the bigger of the other two. The hunk stepped back to make his own challenge on the door but he felt a hand restraining his arm.

It was the seated fellow whom they had passed and who was now standing. 'What the hell you doing?' he demanded. 'You can't go busting in there.'

The big man, wide-eyed at the effrontery of the hand on his arm, gripped its wrist in a massive fist and twisted until the fellow collapsed on the bare boards. 'Stay out of this.'

Having dispensed with the interruption, the big man raised a booted foot and rammed it hard so that the recalcitrant door crashed open. They marched through the gloomy antechamber and into the bedroom.

Already alarmed at the noise outside, a man in the room was standing by the bed trying desperately to negotiate his legs into his trousers. In his haste he had dragged the bed-sheet across the floor so that the young girl had no protection. Hair ruffled, she sat against the backrest, unsuccessfully trying to cover her crotch and breasts with her hands.

The leader of the trio leant against the wall fingering his moustache, amused at the scene. When he had his fill he said, 'Come for the premium, my dear.'

'What premium?' she whimpered.

'For protection.'

'What protection? We don't have to pay for protection. Anyway, my man looks after money and stuff like that.'

The boss nodded back to the stairwell. 'Is that your man back there on the stairs?'

'Yes.'

'Well, your man is indisposed.'

The girl eyed him. 'You're Plug-Uglies, aren't you?'

'And proud of it.'

'Well,' the girl persisted, 'this is Dead Rabbit territory.'

'No, it ain't, missy. *Their* territory ends a block away. So if you are not going to be forthcoming, I opine that we shall have to get the money for ourselves.'

He made a gesture and his men

began ransacking drawers and containers. Meanwhile he crossed to a toilet table; with a pier glass attached it was the only furniture in the room with some elegance. He swept the glass ornaments and perfume from its surface, splintering them on the floor, and yanked out the drawers.

In minutes the threesome had garnered a small collection of bills and coins that were duly handed over to the man with the moustache, who disdainfully considered the small amount in his hand.

'That's all I got,' the girl whimpered.

'Yeah, and it ain't much,' the man observed, before pocketing it. 'Hardly worth the bother.' He turned to the girl's client, who by now had progressed to stuffing his shirt into his trousers. 'But your john here looks like he should be able to make up the deficiency.'

'Have what I got, it's all yours,' the man blurted, emptying his pockets onto the bed.

'And the wallet,' the spokesman said, a heavy threat in his voice.

Suddenly there was a clunk and one of the intruders thumped to the floor, felled by the baseball bat in the hand of a man coming through the doorway. The assailant moved further in and swung the bat at the big man, who sidestepped with a speed surprising for his size.

'I told you to stay out of this,' he snarled, grabbing his attacker's wrists. With little trouble he worked the bat out of the man's hands and picked him up clear of the floor. He bore him through the door and dropped him over the landing rail like he had been nothing more than a sack of garbage. When he returned to the room his downed companion was coming to his feet, nursing his head.

The leader checked that his henchman was all right and looked back at the girl. 'We'll be back next week for the second payment. And tell all your fellow hussies along the street — it's the same for all of them.'

When they got to the lobby downstairs there was a crowd gathering around a still form on the hard tiles.

'He's dead,' somebody said.

The man with the moustache smiled as he pulled on his gloves and stepped out of the building. 'Good. That'll show the others we mean business.'

★　★　★

'The bastards!' The head of the Dead Rabbits looked at his henchman. It had been half an hour since he had received the news but he was still fuming. 'We've had an agreement for bloody years with the Plugs. It was agreed that that stretch of tenements was neutral.'

'You know what it is, boss? Young Dapper Callaghan's flexing his muscles.'

The chief nodded. Despite his diminutive size he was known as the Big Feller, the traditional title for his position. 'No,' he went on, 'it's more than that — he's a frigging headcase.

Always has been. The slimeball. You know, I even shook hands with him at his father's funeral. Biggest funeral Five Points has ever seen. And he deserved it. Mick Callaghan was a man of honour even though he was a Plug-Ugly on the other side of the fence. We had our differences but we settled them amicably. Like that treaty between us and the Plugs marking out the territories.'

'Since his pa died we've lost three men, boss. Snag is they've all been sneak jobs. We can't pin anything on him.'

'It's *four* men. That guy they dropped off the balcony is a distant cousin of my woman's.'

'I didn't know that.'

'Neither did I till my old woman told me. He was only a distant cousin — and she's never had much to do with him — but it still makes him *family*.'

'And that makes it serious,' his henchman said by way of confirmation.

'We gotta do something,' the chief

said, 'but in a gang war we all pay a heavy price.'

'Damn Callaghan,' the other whispered as though to himself. 'He always thought his old man was too soft. Now his pa's gone, he's top dog — and he's seeing how far he can push us. That's about it, boss. You know, pity one of the others in their gang didn't take over when his pa passed on. Okay, they're Plugs but they know the rules.'

The Big Feller raised his hands. 'That's it!' he exclaimed. 'We don't have to have an all-out gang war — we just knock *him* off. The bozo must be just as much a pain in the ass to their mob as he is to us. I figure most of them would thank us for doing him.'

'How do you just . . . knock him off?'

'One man can do it.'

'Johnny Doyle?'

'That's it.' He mused on the idea. 'You know my personal nickname for him? The Expediter.'

'What's an expediter, boss?'

'An expediter? It's somebody who

can get a job done. No messing, just goes in, does a professional job and comes out clean. Put the word out I want to see him.'

★ ★ ★

The Five Points district of Lower Manhattan in the post-Lincoln days of the nineteenth century had certain things in great quantity. Large amounts of drinking, smoking, cheating, fighting, raping, pickpocketing, loft-burgling, prostitution, murdering. It was not a moral place.

To boot, there was a large quantity of starvation and overcrowding. When somebody bothered to count, one room in the infamous tenement block known as the Old Brewery had been found to house over seventy souls. Crammed like rats in a sewer. Consequently, illness was rife — illness without the comfort of doctors in attendance. There was much suffering, dying, bullying, torturing. So neither was it a merry place.

But as Johnny Doyle strutted his way

through the vendors along Orange Street, one thing was without doubt. With all the bustle, shouting, organ-grinders, and appeals by beggars, it was a very busy place.

Like the wretches who made up the population, poverty had once weighed him down; but of late he had lost his vulnerability on that score. For he was a Dead Rabbit. And a very important Dead Rabbit.

Five Points was dominated by Irish gangs and the Dead Rabbits were top of the heap. There were lots of tales of how the gang got its name. But the stories were all folklore. Fact: *ráibéad* was Irish for a big, hulking person and 'dead' meant 'very'. As simple as that. But in combination the two words were enough to strike terror into any who crossed them. Except maybe the Plug-Uglies, the only one of the other gangs big enough to see themselves as a rival.

Back in the old days the place had been the site of a massive pool called The Collect. But garbage and sewage had turned the thing into a cesspool. The authorities had filled it in and built tenements on it. However, in time the buildings began to sink, which accounted for the decrepit look of the area — and the stink. By the mid '80s only the poorest of the poor would countenance living in the place; and Charles Dickens on a visit had observed it was worse than any of the slums he had experienced back in London.

Now the heat of summer made the whole thing worse — heat, stench — and the inhabitants of the Lower East Side had no means of escaping to the country for the season. Not like the uptown nobs.

However, born and raised amidst the squalor, Johnny Doyle was used to it. But there would come a day when he would move to one of the more well-heeled parts of the city. That was his dream. And it had all the possibility of becoming a reality. He was the main troubleshooter for the Dead Rabbits — and the Big Feller paid him well.

Like now for instance, the chief was paying out a heap for him to put the head of the Plug-Uglies out of the way.

His first port of call in the operation was to seek out a certain Declan, one of the fringe figures around the Collect. Although the little guy wasn't a fully paid-up member of the gang the fellow existed on the margin, his speciality being information. Johnny soon came across him leaning against a lamppost at the main intersection of Five Points.

Johnny beckoned for the man to join him down an alleyway out of the way. 'You remember when that Spic was sniffing round your mort,' he began, 'and you wanted him frightened off?'

'Sure thing. I'll never forget you for that. They tell me the buckaroo has still got a limp.' Declan chuckled at the thought.

'And how are things now?' Johnny went on.

'Me and the mort, we wed. Got a couple of nippers now.'

Johnny nodded. 'Family life, can't

beat it.' Then he pushed the conversation in another direction. 'Ain't much happen on the streets you don't know about, eh?'

The other shrugged.

'Well *now* I want you to do me a favour.' He took off his derby, exposing more of his flowing red hair, and extracted a couple of bills from the hat, pushing them into the other's pocket. 'Meanwhiles, that'll help a family man with the grocery bills.' He winked. 'And there'll be more of that when you come up with the goods.'

'Gee, thanks, Johnny. What do you want?'

'You know Dapper?'

'Don't *know* him. 'Course, know *of* him. Head of the Plug-Uglies.'

'That's the guy. I'd like you to tell me everything you know about him. His background. And especially his routine, what he does. Even when he farts, I want to know.'

'No problem, Johnny. Now let me see . . . '

It wasn't long before Johnny had got enough information to formulate a plan. He sought out his partner for the operation. Colm was a young, dependable fellow with whom Johnny regularly worked. He found him playing cards in a speakeasy near the slaughterhouse, expertly fleecing workers who had just come off shift.

Johnny only had to make his presence known, gesture with his eyebrow and Colm dispensed with his card-playing to join him at the bar.

'You know why they call him Dapper?' Johnny said, after he had explained their task. 'Because he dresses all dude-like. Looks after his appearance. Fancy clothes, washes his hair regular. Thinks he's a gent, like back in the old country. And on top of everything else, he lives his life like some goddamn clockwork watch. Does everything regular.'

'That's helpful.'

'Sure is. For instance, every Wednesday he has his hair cut. Spot on eleven. Barbershop on the corner of Canal Street.'

'What about his minders?'

'Got two. And when he goes to the barbershop one goes in with him while the other keeps watch on the sidewalk outside the door.'

Colm nodded as he began to visualize the plan. 'But this one on watch outside, he'll see us coming.'

'Not if we're already *inside*.'

2

It was a more classy joint than Johnny Doyle was used to. Perfumes hung on the air; on the walls were advertisements for brilliantines and varied hair applications. His own hair shearing was normally done by an old granny in the Collect — Granny Mercy — who doubled up as a general sawbones and layer-out of the tenement's dead.

There were two barbers snipping away at a couple of well-to-dos as they entered. One of the tradesmen looked up at his new customers. 'Be with you shortly, gents.'

Johnny walked in between the two chairs and angled his head, this way and that. The occupants were puzzled at his behaviour; they weren't to know he was checking the visibility of the door from the vantage of the chairs.

He nodded silently to Colm, indicating the setup was okay. Moving over to the waiting area against the wall, he noted the time on the banjo-clock on the wall. Some ten minutes to go. 'Don't make it too long,' he said. 'We got important business elsewheres.'

The two sat down to wait and for a while there was just the clip-clip of the scissors with Johnny regularly looking at his watch. At five minutes to go, he nodded to Colm and they stood up.

'Like I said,' Johnny intoned, 'we're in a hurry.' The gangmen pulled the barbers out of the way, swivelled the chairs around and whipped off the sheets from the two customers. 'Pay the man and be on your way without any trouble.'

There was something about the forthright demeanour of the two visitors that pre-empted the notion of causing any 'trouble' — or even voicing opposition.

Johnny and his companion checked the swivel capabilities of the now vacant chairs. Then they dropped into them, threw the sheets around themselves and swivelled to face the mirror. Checking he could see the door, Johnny settled himself into place.

As the haircutting proceeded, the barbers asked no questions or proffered any of the usual while-away-the-time conversation.

Bang on time, two men entered. Johnny slanted an indicative look at his partner. Colm caught the signal, affirmation clear in his eyes, and turned his head casually away giving an almost imperceptible nod.

Johnny drew his own gun under the sheet and looked again at his confederate who nodded in return. Johnny's left hand appeared from under the sheet, just far enough for it to be seen only by his partner, and balled itself into a fist in preparation for the countdown. The index finger sprang stiff, followed by the second finger. On the third, the two men whirled round and fired through the sheets.

The force behind Johnny's slug slammed Dapper Callaghan's head against the wall. The man remained seated, staring with blank eyes.

Simultaneously Colm's round went through the neck of his target and the recipient slumped forward, blood spewing from the ripped-apart artery.

Meantime Johnny had whirled round, altered his aim to line up on the wide-eyed figure approaching the glass of the outer window. His gun cracked a second time, the single bullet delivering two holes — one through the pane, the other into the chest of the outside minder. His target lumbered forward and crashed through the window to splay motionless, half-in, half-out of the establishment. He was probably dead too. But there was no need to check — the Big Feller's point had been made.

Johnny raised a finger to his lips in the direction of the barbers now cringing on the floor. 'You two — stay shtum — or else.' He emphasized his meaning by drawing his flattened palm across his throat and the gunmen sprinted towards the back door, holstering their weapons.

But the door banged open before they reached it — to reveal an ox of a fellow smashing his way in, pistol in hand. Mother Mary — his informant Declan had been wrong. There were *three* minders!

Hearing gunfire and not recognizing the men coming at him, the newcomer triggered his weapon instinctively. Colm spun round and staggered back into the shop. But before the intruder could swing the barrel of his weapon, Johnny's gun was hammering its shots in rapid order, cleaving through flesh and muscle. The man caromed back into the alley.

Johnny dashed to the door, checked there were no more. Back inside he helped the injured Colm to his feet. He pulled his partner's arm over his shoulder and heaved the man outside.

There was a youth standing wide-eyed in the alley. Johnny took some coins and pushed them into the lad's hands. 'Don't worry, the shooting's all over. Get in there smart. Tell the barber damages will be paid for by the Big Feller. But stress, that's as long as he don't grass on us to the crushers. And make it clear what will happen if he does spill anything.'

And with that he began to manoeuvre his human burden down the alley. 'It's Granny Mercy for you, boyo,' he whispered, 'to get some dressing on that scratch.'

When he was well clear of the scene he pondered on the mishap. He had a reputation for a clean job, for things not going wrong. But he decided against blaming Declan. The extra minder would have been laid on because of the possibility of trouble brewing. Johnny mentally kicked himself; he should have anticipated that himself. He had simply allowed himself to be distracted by the tested reliability of his informant.

★　★　★

The Big Feller's organization was an octopus with tentacles all over the East

Side so that by the time Johnny reported, his chief knew of the killings.

'You done a good job,' the overlord said, pushing the promised wad of bills across the table.

Johnny hefted the weight in his hand before slipping it into his pocket. 'Thanks, boss. Pity Colm caught one. But Old Granny Mercy says he won't be laid low for long.'

'Maybe you should lie low, too.'

Johnny's shrugged dismissively.

'I mean it,' the Dead Rabbit leader grunted. 'You know we don't own the police any more?'

That was true. The City Police Department had been so under the influence of the gangs that it had eventually been disbanded and the Metropolitan Police had been created in its place with the intention of having a clean force.

'Yeah.'

'Well, Johnny me lad, the new lot may come looking for you — and I can't stop 'em. So far they all got clean noses.'

He leant across and tugged at the younger man's red chin whiskers. 'You might start by fetching that off. Doesn't quite help you to fit into the crowd.' Then he nodded to the bulge in Johnny's jacket. 'And you could use that extra dough to take yourself away someplace until the heat cools off.'

'Where would I go? I've never been outside New York in my life. Besides, you know, Manhattan is a warren. I keep my head down, keep off the streets, the law will never find me in a month of Sundays.'

'Times are changing, Johnny. I don't think it's going to be that easy any more. Take it from me, you really need to consider clearing out for a spell. Buffalo, or Chicago, maybe.'

'OK, boss, I'll give it some thought. Be seeing you, Big Feller.'

The gang chief stuck out his hand. 'Thanks again, Johnny — and watch yourself.'

Buffalo, Chicago? he mused as he clunked down the stairs. Who did he know in Buffalo or Chicago? Or anywhere else out of town for that matter. Where could he go? Where would he *want* to go?

Outside he headed for his usual speakeasy. He needed to unwind with a drink and a game of cards. He paused at the sidewalk kerb to allow the incoming mail-coach to pass. Then he crossed the road, oblivious to the fact that aboard that very conveyance was something of great significance to him. Something that would answer his question.

⋆　⋆　⋆

Hours later he was feeling real good. Replete with Irish stout he was finishing off an already profitable day with a pile of poker winnings in front of him.

'Johnny, you ma's calling for you.' Tugging at his elbow was one of the young street urchins who were used as runners.

'Ma? What's she want at this time of night?'

'Dunno. Just passing on the message.'

He gathered his winnings, slipping a coin to the deliverer. 'Thanks.'

Up in the squalid tenement that his mother called home, the first interpretation he made of the scene that met him was that his mother was ill. Eyes red and closed, cheekbones wet, she was lying flat out with several women in attendance around her bed.

'Oh, Johnny,' she whimpered when one of the women informed her of his entrance. He crossed to her side and she grabbed at him.

'What is it, Ma?' he asked.

Without speaking she held up a piece of paper crushed in her hand. He broke free of her clutches and took the missive to one of the oil-lamps on the wall. He smoothed it out. Postmarked five weeks since, it was a letter from some girl in Sangrano, Arizona Territory notifying the death of Brendan, his brother. No details, just that he'd passed away. He returned to the bed and cradled his mother. 'Oh, Ma.'

'Oh, Brendan, Brendan,' she moaned. Then she wiped her eyes. 'Johnny, you must go. I'm too frail for such a journey.'

He couldn't see the point of anybody going. The time that it had taken for the letter to cross the country his brother would have been long since put under the sod. And where the blue hell was Sangrano? Come to that where the blue hell was Arizona?

'You must go,' she continued. 'Pay the proper respects in my stead. See that his grave's fitting and that he had a good Catholic funeral. Lay some flowers.'

He didn't question his mother's instructions. In the old way it was simply his duty to obey. He stayed with his distraught mother until the early hours.

* * *

Back in his room he thought on the matter. There was a little sadness in his heart; but only a little, and no tears in his eyes. The two brothers had never been close; and he hadn't seen his elder sibling for years.

Brendan had been born in the old country. That's probably why they were chalk and cheese. They had looked alike — both had the same chiselled face and red-tinged hair — but physical featuring was the end of the similarity. Brendan was a straight-up fellow working in the slaughterhouse and didn't take to his younger brother's wild life, stealing and taking up with the gangs. Maybe their difference in outlook was because Brendan had been brought up in the old ways — to know your place in the scheme of things, touch your forelock to your betters.

Huh, the only man Johnny rated as his better was the man who could floor him; and even then he wouldn't acknowledge superiority until he'd got up and been whacked down enough times for him not to be able to get up again. Born and bred in the dog-eat-dog world of New York he hadn't been schooled in the old ways.

Nor had he known about open spaces, fields and growing your own food. Which is why he didn't understand his brother's restlessness in the confines of the city and why he always rambled on about being at one with nature; and why he finally left the city to find *another* Ireland, a better Ireland, out West.

Huh, fat lot of good it had done him.

3

The stagecoach swung to one side as its wheels hit an awkward road rut then resumed its regular bouncing.

'You ain't from these parts.' The speaker was a solid-shouldered cattleman, skin like leather, a Stetson on the seat beside him.

'No.'

There was nothing invitational in the response but the other persevered. 'Back East from the look of your duds and the sound of your talk.'

The speaker was mighty astute to draw conclusions from the other's speech as the man had hardly said anything throughout the trip.

'Got some Irish in there, I suspect. Red hair and all.'

No response.

'Scandinavian myself,' the first speaker continued, reconciling himself to the fact that he was talking to himself. 'Least-ways my folks' folks were from Sweden.'

The stage bumped on a few more miles during which the cattleman observed his silent travelling companion some more. Eventually, he said, 'As we're getting close to town, I hope you don't mind me giving you a piece of advice, mister.'

Johnny Doyle took his gaze from the window but didn't comment. A long train journey, a seemingly longer period having his teeth shaken to their roots by stagecoach. He'd had enough.

'It's mighty wild country out here,' the other went on. 'Ain't no law for a hundred miles. A genteel Easterner might find folk mighty tough.'

'Is that so?'

'And they don't take kindly to strangers. If you're aiming to stay in town a spell it'd be to your advantage to buy some range gear. That way, at least you won't stand out like a greenhorn ripe for some razzing. Otherwise you could run into trouble with the local yahoos the moment you step into the street.'

The other returned his eyes to the passing scenery. Then, after a dragged-out spell, said, 'Listen, mister. I'm sure you're being kind in passing on your observations but I make it a rule to always expect the worst from folks. I find it works.'

★   ★   ★

Johnny stood flat-footed on the dirt that was the main street of Sangrano. At the far end the stage was being circled in preparation to receive a new team for its return journey. He wiped the sweat from his brow and took in the town, a spread of adobes centred on a nucleus of wooden-frame buildings.

A few moments on he could detect a rumble and folks began leaving the street. Riders untied their horses from hitch rails and hastily led them into alleys. Then he saw why, as cattle came careering round the corner. He grabbed his valise and dived for the boardwalk to take refuge in the doorway of a dress-store.

It only took a few seconds for the small bunch to thunder past and they were gone as quickly as they came, the pound of hoofs fading. An elderly lady with a newly purchased bundle and seemingly unperturbed by the event, squeezed past him.

'Does that happen often, ma'am?' he asked.

'What? Oh, that. Occasionally. It's only open-range beef taking it upon themselves to take a wander round town.'

She continued on her shopping route as he looked down at the dust that clung to him like a grey shroud.

He patted himself down, picked up his valise and made for the first building he saw with the word HOTEL over it. After a wash and a meal, he asked for directions to the funeral parlour.

★ ★ ★

The place had a smell Johnny didn't like.

'You buried Brendan Doyle?'

The black-suited undertaker repeated the name, reflecting on it.

'You sent notification to his ma in New York,' Johnny reminded him. 'That's why I'm here.'

'Ah, yes. I remember now. Charity case.'

'Charity case?'

'There was no one to pay his bills. There's twenty dollars owing on his burying.'

'So where's he buried?'

'Like I said, there's twenty dollars to pay.'

'Twenty dollars? That's a hell of a sum. What'd you do — build him a pillared tomb?'

'Timber's scarce in these parts.'

Johnny grabbed him by the lapels and pulled him close. 'Listen, coffin-man, I'm his brother and I didn't come two thousand miles to dicker or chew the fat. Where's he buried?'

'Town cemetery, just out of town.'

Johnny pushed him away. 'What did he die of?'

'Some kind of accident.'

'Accident?'

'Something to do with falling off a horse, if I recall. Listen, I'm no doctor, mister. I just bury 'em.'

'And where's the town boneyard?'

'West of town, half a mile.'

Johnny turned on his heel. He paused at the door and drew a couple of bills from his wad. He balled them up and dropped them on the floor before stepping outside.

At the edge of town he took off his hat and used it to fan his face.

A gaggle of old-timers were throwing horse-shoes. One noted the lone figure in the middle of the drag. 'Say, fellows. Wonder what the Prince of Wales is doing out here?' His companions looked up and laughed.

Johnny ignored them and wiped his brow. He didn't know about Wales but — blue hell — this place was sure hotter than New York in a heatwave. He replaced his hat and began the trudge along the trail.

The cemetery was unfenced, just a scattering of wooden and stone markers. Brendan's last resting place was on the edge of the plot. A mound and two staves tacked together in the shape of a cross. He took off his hat and studied the roughly hacked letters. Had the carver spelt Doyle right? Not being a reading man he wasn't sure. But it was of no matter.

'It's my reckoning you're Johnny.'

He was momentarily startled by the voice. So concentrated had he been on his task he had not heard anyone arrive. He turned to see a young woman. At least she had the voice and figure of a woman but she looked strange dressed in whipcord pants. New York women didn't wear trousers.

'Johnny Doyle if I'm not mistaken,' she went on.

'That's the truth of it, ma'am. How did you know?'

'The grave you're looking at. Your duds. And the look of you. Now I can see your face, I'm sure.'

'You knew Brendan?'

'Yes, and he spoke much of you.'

He worked his hat-brim through his fingers. 'You have the advantage of me, ma'am.'

'Mary Blanchard.'

'Mary, a pretty name. You were Brendan's girlfriend?'

'Kind of. More friends really, nothing serious. We saw each other now and again; enjoyed each other's company.' She looked back at the grave. 'I'm sorry for disturbing you. I'll leave you with your thoughts.'

Johnny shrugged. 'I've paid my respects.'

The girl considered him for a moment, then said: 'Listen, I'm just going into town to purchase some supplies. There's a restaurant there. If you're a gentleman like Brendan — as I'm sure you are — you could buy me a coffee and we could talk. I've heard so much about you.'

'Don't know about that gentleman thing, ma'am, but I'd be honoured to buy you refreshment.'

A quarter-hour on they were taking their time over a pot of coffee. Johnny noted how her lightbrown hair, sun-bleached in streaks, was pulled back to a neat bun at the back. 'If you forgive me, miss,' he said, 'and allow me to speak openly. You are a comely lass and my brother had eyes in his head. As a consequence I have difficulty in under-standing why you and he were not in closer relation.'

'He saw no temptation to be otherwise. Yes, he was attracted to me. Indeed, the attraction was mutual. But he was an honest man and made it clear that he would not press his suit until he could afford to maintain me from his own resources. I told him that did not matter. That we could get by. But he insisted on gathering enough money about him to get us started.'

'That's our Brendan. As straight as they come.'

They exchanged some more snippets, then she asked, 'How long are you staying?'

'I've got no plans. See, it was Ma who sent me out here. She's too old to make the journey herself and pay her respects. Well, I've seen Brendan's grave and got something to tell Ma, which is what I came for, so there's nothing to keep me here.' He mused for a moment. 'On the other hand, it's taken me several weeks to get out here so I've a mind to rest up a spell before heading back.'

'In that case you may want to have a few words with Jonas, Brendan's friend. He could tell you more about Brendan's life out here — more bits and pieces that you could pass on to your mother.'

He contemplated the suggestion. 'Yeah, figure Ma would like that. Who's this Jonas?'

'Jonas Hill. Brendan's buddy out at the Slash S.'

'Slash S?'

'Monte Manzoni's outfit up north. That's where Brendan worked as a ranch hand.'

'How do I get out there?'

'Hire a horse from the livery stable.'

He laughed. 'And what would I do with a horse? I'm a city boy.'

'You can't ride?'

'I can't ride.'

She nodded. 'That does present an obstacle.'

He looked out of the window at the gig. 'That contraption back there, would it be a presumption to ask you to take me out there in it? I'd make it worth your time.'

She shook her head. 'There's no proper trail to the spread. You will note that the wheels are delicate. They wouldn't take the rough ground.' She considered further. 'I have an idea. I could teach you how to sit in a saddle along with some elementary rein skills. Then I could accompany you out there to make sure you didn't get into trouble.'

He chuckled quietly.

'What's funny?'

'The notion of me in a saddle.'

'Well?'

'Indeed, ma'am. I accept your kind invitation.'

'Where are you staying?'

He pondered. 'I think it's called the Republic.'

'Yes, I know the Republic Hotel. Now horse riding is not something you learn in five minutes so we need to start early. So I'll pick you up . . . say seven in the morning?'

4

He looked back, stifling an early-morning yawn. The town, the only sign of humanity, had now disappeared over the skyline. 'It's kind of remote out here. Don't you miss company?'

She laughed as she flicked the ribbons of the gig. 'Oh, bless you, we have company.'

'Such as?'

'Jackrabbits, hummingbirds, mountain lions, rattlesnakes.'

'I mean human.'

She pointed south. 'Mexican border's ten miles thataways. So we're on a North-South route.'

'I don't see a road.'

'It's the kind of traffic that doesn't need a road. Smugglers — both ways. Then there's the rustling. Cattle rustled in Mexico are driven north. On the other hand cattle rustled in the States

are herded south.' She chuckled. 'Can
be real chaotic at times when they run
into each other. And there are always
outlaws. Just like the cattle, they move
in both directions.'

'Ain't you scared with outlaws
around?'

'We got guns, of course. But the
runaways are in too much of a hurry to
bother us. We get travellers knocking
regular on the door for water. They've
never threatened us. We have some
conversation, they tell us where they've
come from and where they're heading.
Pack of lies of course but it passes the
time of day.'

'What about the crushers?'

'Crushers?'

'The law. Don't they bother with all
these shenanigans?'

'There are border patrols. But they're
short on manpower and it's a mighty
long border. Sometimes we hear gunfire
in the distance, usually at night, when
we guess somebody's been sighted.
They do say there's somebody on this

side of the border controlling a lot of the operations, but that's just rumour.'

Unnecessarily he ducked as a shadow darkened the buggy for a second. A vulture had flown low over their heads to join its fellows, squarking and gawking in a circle in the scrub.

'Probably a left-over deer carcass,' she observed and pointed ahead. 'Look, nearly there.'

The homestead was set way off the trail and backing onto a small wood.

'You're lucky to be visiting the territory late summer. Been a bad drought this year. Well was almost dry. Summer storms came late. But now the ponds are filling up and the place is getting green again.'

They rolled past a vegetable field and approached the several buildings that constituted her home, scattering chickens as they neared.

'See,' she said, pointing west as she reined in. 'Mount Wrightson. You can just see it from here.'

He stepped down and out of

politeness squinted in the indicated direction. Between two uplands he could just make out a blue triangle in the distance. He tried to show interest but he wasn't bothered. He'd seen the first mountain of his life through the train window on the journey out. But once you've seen one mountain you've seen them all.

Hearing the buggy, an old man working in a vegetable field looked up.

'There's only me and Pa now,' she said. 'Ma passed on some ten years ago. And Pa, he's a bit — you know — in his old age.'

'Never knew my pa,' Johnny said. 'The rugheaded kern upped sticks just after I came into the world. Left Ma tending to me and Brendan all by herself. Never seen him as I know of. Fact is, the only thing I *do* know of him is that he had red hair — oh, and he liked the horses.'

'This is Johnny Doyle, Pa,' she called as the oldster emerged from the patch with a bunch of carrots and headed towards the house. 'Brendan's brother.'

The man dragged a game leg across the hardened earth, wiped his hand on his overalls and shook the hand of the visitor. 'Mighty glad to meet you son,' he said after he'd relayed his condolences. He stepped back and eyed their visitor. 'My, must say you sure look like your brother.'

'Now leave him be, Pa,' Mary said, taking the carrots and ripping off a handful. 'We haven't got time to dilly-dally. I told you we have some serious riding to do.'

'Come on, tenderfoot,' she said, turning and walking towards a barn with a corral skirting its front. He followed her in, clambering over the fence and towards the stable door. Light cascaded into the building as she opened the door. 'Morning, my beauties,' she said, approaching the stalls.

There were two horses and their ears swivelled in response to the familiar voice, their heads appearing over the rails. She gave them each a welcoming stroke, then slipped the latches and the animals trotted out into the morning sun.

Johnny watched them canter round the perimeter. Having worked the sleep out of their muscles the animals halted before the girl. She stroked the attention-seeking noses and gave them a carrot each.

'That's the one,' she said pointing to the darker of the two. She handed one of the remaining carrots to Johnny. 'Feed him so he'll see you as a friend.'

With some trepidation the man, whose only savvy was that of the streets, held out the vegetable.

She laughed at the sight. 'Don't be frightened. Didn't you inherit any of your father's horse skills at all? You said he was a horse man.'

'He used to *bet* on 'em, ma'am, not *ride* 'em.'

Eventually the animal got the whole of his carrot from the reluctant deliverer and proceeded to crunch in a lazy way.

'We call him Walker,' she went on. 'Never been known to run. Used to be Pa's horse but Pa took a fall and hasn't took to riding since. So he's a well-schooled horse and used to being ridden. Figure he'll relish the exercise. He'll get you anywhere — provided you're in no hurry.'

At her suggestion Johnny disrobed, draping his jacket over a post with his derby on the top of it.

'Right,' she said when he returned. 'Now, we're going to start with you playing games with the horse.'

'Playing games? You said you were going to give me the rudiments of riding.'

She smiled and shook her head. 'We're not going to be able to rush this, city boy. We've got to get rid of any tension in the two of you. You'll be able to sense how he moves while he'll learn not to see you as a threat.'

He did as he was bid, running alongside the horse, teasing it with a carrot, stroking it and letting the animal nudge him. After a while he stopped, bent over with his hands on his knees and took heavy breaths.

'OK, city boy,' she said as he wiped his brow. 'I can see it's time for a break and lemonade.'

Half an hour later, they were back in the corral and the girl had saddled his mount-to-be.

'Normally you'd have the reins in your hand while mounting,' she said, 'but I'll hold them until you're used to it.'

She motioned for him to mount.

He hesitated. Suddenly the horse looked a lot taller. She nodded for him to grip the saddle horn and put his foot in the stirrup. He did so but the point of his foot stuck in the horse's flank and it stepped sideways so that he hopped in pursuit, one foot up in the air.

'Sorry about that,' she said as she got the animal under control again. 'I forgot to tell you. When you mount up, turn the stirrup out so you can slip your foot in easily without disturbing the horse.'

After he had successfully settled in the saddle she let him acclimatize to the feel, then said, 'I'm going to lead the horse for you so you can get used to the saddle and both of you can get used to each other. Allow yourself to be part of the horse's movement.'

After several circuits she stopped. 'You've got to learn how to relax in the saddle. If you're tense the horse will feel tense and also tense itself against any discomfort you're causing and thus make it difficult to control.'

'I can't help being tense.'

'Yes, you can. You're a big boy now. Have you done much dancing?'

'Yes.'

'I mean close to a woman.'

'I've done my share.'

'Well, this is the same. Yours and the horse's movements must be co-ordinated in a natural way, just like dancing. And talk to your horse.'

'Sweet nothings like on the dance floor?'

'If you like.'

After another hour they took a second break. 'Don't dismount leaving one foot in the stirrup like that,' she advised as she watched him. 'If the horse moves off you're gonna fall back before you can release your foot and you can be dragged.'

Come the afternoon he was riding slowly around the corral unaided.

'Remember,' she said from her position of sitting on the pole-fence, 'your hands and reins are not the means of steering. The main way of steering the horse is through your legs and weight. Ever been to a rodeo?'

'No, ma'am. Like you keep reminding me — I'm a city boy.'

'Well if you had been to a Western show you would have seen some riders completing very complicated manoeuvres with no bridle or reins.'

'Bully for them.'

By evening he had ridden two times round the mile perimeter of the homestead following Mary, very slowly but unaided. When they settled on the porch with her father after supper, there was a distinct shine on the seat of his pants and aching in his buttocks; but he was quietly pleased with his achievement.

5

Mary rode into town at sun-up the next day with Walker in tow. Johnny was waiting for her on the hotel veranda, munching cheese and bread that he had chivvied out of the yawning cook who hadn't yet fired up his breakfast stove.

The early sunlight was cool and they headed out at a steady walking gait with Mary in the lead. Just as she had said, Walker was a docile animal, happy to follow her a few paces to the rear with little instruction from its greenhorn rider — who still had enough to do getting used to the hard leather rubbing at his backside.

In time the rising sun in a cloudless sky began to take its toll while the wind drifting across the flats made the heat seem more torrid.

Eventually they crossed a tree-lined stream bed and topped a gentle rise to see the two-storey frame house that marked the ranch headquarters. Around it lay a configuration of adobe and log outbuildings. Hitting a wagon track they followed it around a tack barn, to come in sight of a bunkhouse and sundry shacks.

'*Buenos dias*,' Mary said to a group of straw-hatted Mexican hands who were resetting a corral post. 'Jonas Hill,' she said after an exchange of greeting. 'We're looking for Jonas Hill.'

'Ah, Señnor Jonas,' one said and pointed to the nearest building. 'He is in the bunkhouse, *señorita*. I will take you.'

They dismounted, accepting the offer of another worker to tend to their horses, and followed the first speaker. He tapped at the door, opened it and announced the visitors. Then he stepped aside gesturing with his hand for them to enter. There were around a dozen bunks and in the aisle between them a Mexican woman busied herself collecting linen. One man was sitting at a table playing solitaire while another lounged on a bunk. Against the wall there was a large leather settee with rents from which straw poked. The smell of coffee came from a pot bubbling on a stove.

The man on the bunk rose. He was a squarejawed man with the leathery skin that attested to much contact with wind and weather. 'Miss Mary, what brings you out here?'

Mary introduced her companion.

'Jonas Hill, at your service, sir,' the man said, shaking Johnny's hand. 'Yeah, I was a workmate of your brother. He was the kind of buddy a guy has time for. He's gonna be sadly missed.' For a moment reminiscence reflected in his eyes. 'Him and his Irish blarney.'

'How did it happen?' Johnny asked.

'Fell from his horse out on the range. It was a box valley and the beef was acting up. Before anyone could get to him he'd been trampled. Not the best way to go but it happens.'

He crossed to the stove. 'I'm forgetting my manners. Figure you weary travellers could do with some refreshment.'

They thanked him. He wiped out some chipped tin mugs and filled them. He indicated for them to sit on the settee and pulled up a rickety chair to join them. They spoke for a while with Jonas relating a selection of recollections, the trivial incidents that make up a working life. The man at the table reflectively turning over the pasteboards seemingly had little interest in the exchange.

Suddenly a look of unease clouded Jonas's features and he said, 'Excuse me, folks, must use the privy out back.'

On his return the couple had drained their mugs and were standing in preparation to leave.

'Thank you for sparing the time,' Johnny said. 'It was good to talk to someone who knew Brendan.'

They shook hands once more, then the cowpuncher said, 'Before you go — you may as well take something that belonged to your brother.'

He crossed to a chest and took out a small burlap parcel. He brought it over and revealed a small Bible. 'May as well have this. Nobody round here has much use for it.' In the motion of returning it to its wrapping he winked at Johnny and appeared to slip something between the pages.

'Thanks,' Johnny said, taking the package. 'His ma will appreciate having something of his.' He'd already noted the cowman's apprehensive glance thrown in the direction of the fellow playing solitaire.

Outside they were watering the horses in preparation for their return when Jonas came alongside. Surreptitiously he tapped the parcel, which was still in Johnny's hand, and whispered, 'An hour.'

Johnny looked at him but the man shook his head silently, indicating that he should not react. And over Jonas's shoulder he saw the solitaire man now watching from the doorway of the bunkhouse. Johnny flicked his eyes in

56

acknowledgment of the need for subterfuge and posited the book in a saddlebag. He buckled it and untied the reins. They made their goodbyes and mounted up.

★ ★ ★

When they were out of sight of the ranch, Johnny shouted to his companion to pull in. With the horses at a standstill he eased himself down. He took the Bible from his saddlebag and extracted the note. The lettering had the appearance of being hastily scrawled with a stubby pencil.

'Split Oak in an hour,' he read out loud and passed it to the girl.

'What's the Split Oak?' he asked.

She read it for herself, then pointed west. 'There's a dried-out creek that-aways. It's dominated by an old oak that looks like it must have been hit by lightning years back.'

Johnny retrieved the paper. 'That's why our Mr Hill made a show of going to the privy,' he concluded. 'It was to write this message. I thought it was ungallant for him to use such a word in the presence of a lady. At the time I put it down to manners being less sophisticated out here in the wilds.'

She shook her head. 'You've got a lot to learn, Mr Doyle. It's my understanding that, if anything, the rights and wrongs of etiquette are even stronger out here.'

'Well, either way, his subterfuge means this is important. Any idea what it means?'

She shook her head.

He read it again. 'An hour,' he repeated. 'That's what he whispered to me as we were mounting up.'

She nodded. 'Yes, it's quite clear he has something to tell you that he didn't want the rest to know.'

He slipped the paper into his pocket. 'Yeah, especially that shifty-eyed kern playing cards. Wonder what it's all about. Well, lead the way, ma'am.'

Half an hour on they espied the tree

in the distance. Half-blasted away, the remnants of the plant gave the appearance of a giant, scrawny hand, like arthritic fingers groping at some unseen object.

Reaching it they circled the comb of the creek. They reined in and hitched their mounts to scrub. Johnny took a watch from his vest pocket and checked the time. Then he stretched and, slowly, methodically, rubbed his muscles. Weariness bit into his very bones — weariness born of hours in the saddle. Not a long trip for an experienced saddleman, but for a greenhorn another matter.

Mary laughed when his attention turned to his backside which he had begun to caress gently with his eyes closed. Not appreciating the humour he lit a cigarette and looked back at the way they had come.

Then they took refuge from the heat under the tree. He lay down and put his hat over his eyes. Even with the background buzz of insects, to metropolitan ears there was an impression of silence.

That is until, after a while, the girl spoke. 'What do you do back there in New York?'

He thought about what answer he should give. 'I'm an odd-job man.'

'Doing what exactly?'

'Jobs that are odd,' he said with a chuckle.

She let the words hang in the air, then asked, 'This the first time you've been out West, isn't it?'

'It's the first time I've been out of New York.'

'Must be a great change for you.'

'You can say that again, lady.'

'You say that as though your opinion is unfavourable.'

'It's the kind of world that Brendan wanted but it's not for me. I miss hard paving under my feet, the bustle of folk everywhere.'

He slipped his hat away from his face and wiped his brow. He looked with wrinkled nose at flies that were cutting figures of eight around some droppings close by, then he squinted into the distance — a wilderness to the horizon. 'Heat,' he observed, 'miles between places, no folk, crazy cattle all over the place. Jeez.'

He looked at his watch, his mind on the matter in hand. 'Where can that Jonas be?'

'There must be some attractions to life out here that you've noticed,' she persisted.

He shook his head. 'None that I can see.' Then, 'Fresh air, maybe. That's a novelty to a guy like me.'

'There you are. There is something about the place that appeals.'

Her strange anxiety that he should like the alien land irritated him. 'I'm very fond of desserts,' he said, 'especially canned peaches. But I don't want to eat them all the time.' And he returned to a horizontal position with his hat back over his eyes.

She gave up and went down to the horses. The animals made better conversation.

It was over an hour when they

spotted a speck in the distance coming over a ridge. Eventually they could make out a lone rider heading in the direction they had come.

'Looks like him,' Johnny said, stepping up to some high ground so that he could be more easily seen. He was about to wave when the rider keeled out of the saddle. A split second later the sound of a rifle crack whanging across the flats reached their ears.

'Jesus,' Johnny mouthed. Instinctively he grabbed Mary and pulled her to the ground. He looked back to check their horses couldn't be seen.

'Keep out of sight,' he whispered and eased himself up. He could make out two riders coming down from the ridge. Reaching the fallen figure they dismounted. Then he heard another shot. Seconds later the two were heading back the way they had come.

'What was that?' Mary asked from her lower position.

'The bastards shot him again,' he grunted. 'At close range.'

She inched up, just in time to see the riders disappear over the ridge. For a moment she studied the still figure in the middle distance. 'We have to see how bad he is.'

'Don't hold out any hope, lady. He's beyond help. That last shot was a deliberate killing shot.'

She slumped back, face white. 'What shall we do?' Then, 'We'll have to ride into town and tell the sheriff.'

'I'm not leaving the fellow out there,' he said. 'We'll take him in.'

'But what about the bushwhackers? They may be waiting.'

'Don't think so. They didn't see us — and they've cleared off. It should be safe enough. You stay here while I check.'

It was the first time he had ridden alone but he was getting into the habit of guiding with his body and the bridle-wise animal caused him no trouble. As he neared he recognized Jonas from the bunkhouse. And he had been right. After the first shot, which had hit the shoulder, there had been a shot to the forehead.

He looked about him and saw Jonas's horse grazing in the distance. With his deficiency in horse skills, there was no point in trying to retrieve the animal. He heaved the body across his saddle and began walking the horse back to the tree. He was met by Mary riding out to him. She winced as she saw the bloodied body. 'I'll see if I can rope his horse,' she said and cantered out in the direction of the riderless steed.

Johnny stopped his walk and watched her successfully capture the mount. He transferred the body to the man's own horse.

'I'm sorry to ask, but could you tow Jonas?' he asked as she joined him. 'I don't know whether I could handle two horses yet.'

'Of course,' she said.

She took the reins of the dead man's horse and tied them to the cantle. 'Do you think that this has anything to do with our visit?'

He bent down, wrenched up a bunch of sundried grass and used it to wipe away the blood that now adorned his own saddle. 'Jonas here was going to tell us something about Brendan. Seeings as they were prepared to kill him to prevent him talking to us, it's got to be something serious. That means it has be about Brendan's death. Maybe it wasn't the accident everybody makes out.' He thought some more. 'Seems there's something wrong with that Slash S outfit. Who did you say was the top man?'

'Monte Manzoni.'

'Maybe he's behind it.'

He mounted up and the sorry-looking trio of horses headed back towards town.

'Being brung up on the East River I been smelling rats all my life,' he said after a few yards. 'And I can smell one now.'

6

In town they went straight to the law office and Johnny identified himself to the sheriff. The lawman came out to inspect the body and they went inside, where Johnny explained what had happened.

Sheriff Quince was a tall man of later years with an easy manner and he listened with an alertness in his eye. When the telling had finished, he looked at the banjo-clock on the wall. 'Sure is a bad business. Anyways, it's a long ways out there and it's too late today to do anything. I'll ride out tomorrow and do some investigating.'

'You want me to come?' Johnny offered.

'No need. I know where the Split Oak is and you've given a precise location of the attack. I'll do some poking around, see what I can find, then mosey out to the Slash S and do some questioning there, see what they know.'

A perturbed look crossed Johnny's features. 'But if it's hands from the ranch that are responsible for this killing they're not going to admit to it, are they?'

'Just leave it with me, sir.'

There was something in the way he pronounced the 'sir' which irritated Johnny. 'Listen, Sheriff, we are talking about two deaths here. Two deaths which are clearly linked.'

'There's nothing clear about it. Your brother's was an accident. That was the conclusion of the coroner. This shooting today is a separate matter. It requires investigation, of course. But as to these ideas about the Slash S being involved — Mr Manzoni even — that's what in the business we call hearsay.'

'Yeah, but it could give you a lead.'

The lawman shrugged. 'Maybe.'

'Something more needs to be done than asking a few questions.'

'Such as what?'

'I don't know. You're the sheriff.'

The easy-going manner changed. 'Exactly. I'm the sheriff. Now, you've explained what happened, you've done your civic duty. You've told me what you've heard and what you suspect. Now you leave it to me.' He stood up and walked towards the door and opened it to usher them out. As he did so his eye fell on the forlorn carcass. 'Meantimes, son, I'd be obliged if you could get the deceased over to the funeral parlour. You know where that is?'

'I know where it is.'

Once more outside with the door closed behind them, Johnny looked up and down the street in unseeing exasperation. 'Damn crushers,' he mouthed. 'When you don't want them they're breathing down your neck — and when you do, they got no interest.' He wasn't concerned about Jonas Hill. The fellow had seemed a regular enough guy but Johnny didn't know him. Nor was he concerned about the man's death. He had been close to death many times — indeed, he had caused a number of them in his young life. But he was concerned that everything pointed to somebody having killed his brother. And if that was the case, then somebody needed fingering and wiping out. And Jonas's death was a connection in the whole business.

At the funeral parlour the undertaker noted the freight lying across the saddle and beckoned Johnny to bring it. 'This way.'

Johnny eased the body down, stooped and heaved it over his shoulder. The man led the way through the parlour into a back room and gestured to a table. Johnny lowered the remains onto the surface.

'He got any relatives you know of?' he asked Mary.

'Not that I know of. But I didn't know him that well.'

'All the same,' Johnny said, starting to go through Jonas's pockets, 'I'd better take his belongings in case someone comes claiming.'

'And if he's got no kin who's gonna be paying?' the undertaker wanted to know.

Amongst the dead man's bric-a-brac was three dollars fifty. 'How much?' Johnny asked.

The man looked the corpse up and down in a cold, professional manner. 'Figure I can do this young man for, say, ten dollars.'

'You hornswoggler,' Mary chided. 'You charged us *twenty* for Brendan.'

'Charged *you*?' Johnny queried.

'Yes. Jonas and I chipped in together to meet the bill.'

'And,' Johnny growled, grabbing the man's lapel, 'you charged me the same amount for the *same* bill.'

'I was forgetting,' the man whimpered. 'Genuine mistake.'

'Yeah,' Johnny muttered, pushing the man away and sticking out his hand.

The man pulled the requisite number of bills out of his wallet and handed them over.

'Sorry, mister.'

Johnny handed back ten. 'That's to cover our friend Jonas here.'

With that he moved towards the exit but the undertaker noticed he'd left the change from the deceased's pockets alongside the body. He picked it up and followed after the couple. 'Excuse me, mister, you left this.'

'Yeah, I left it deliberately,' Johnny grunted. 'On account.'

'On account of what?'

'On account of if you cause me any more trouble you'll need another box,' he snapped. 'For yourself.'

Outside he came to a standstill at the edge of the boardwalk, leant on the rail and looked at Jonas's mount. 'Can you use a horse and rig, ma'am?'

'No.'

'Well, we'll sell it and split the difference between us. It'll help reimburse us on all these funeral expenses we keep paying out.'

⋆　⋆　⋆

Early next morning he stationed himself near the law office to monitor events and saw the sheriff leave. It was around eleven and it was plain the man didn't seem in any great rush. Johnny sat on a boardwalk chair and watched the town go about its business. He returned to the hotel and killed time lying on his bed till lunchtime. After his meal he went outside and took up residence once more in a boardwalk chair.

Mid-afternoon he saw the sheriff ride back into town. Unless the lawman was a quick worker, there didn't seem to have been time for much investigating. He followed the man to his office to learn of any developments. There weren't any. The sheriff had found no leads at the scene of the killing. He related his interrogations at the ranch and that the hands knew nothing of the incident.

'Of course they'll say they know nothing,' Johnny retorted. 'I told you. What did you expect?'

'Listen, son, I've done all I can do. I'm one man and it's a big bailiwick.'

Back on the boardwalk, Johnny leant on a rail, sighing in exasperation. Being stymied was a strange feeling for him. Up to this time in his life he'd always known what to do, who to ask, who knew what. He knew the nooks and crannies — where to hole up, where to get the jump on somebody. He knew the people, those whom he could trust, those whom he couldn't. But this was not the Lower East Side. In this alien environment he was a fish out of water; and he didn't like it.

He needed time to think. In the meantime, he would mix, keep his own counsel and listen. Maybe he could pick up some useful scuttlebutt himself.

To this end, after his evening meal, he went on a tour of the saloons. The first one he entered — sporting the simple name Logans — displayed a contrast with even the most wretched speakeasy with which he was familiar back in New York. The floor was hard-packed earth. Behind the bar was a faint, marked-out rectangle where there'd clearly been the traditional mirror. It was also clear by the discolouration of the space that there hadn't been a mirror in place for a long, long time. Probably wasn't worth anybody's while replacing it.

He bought a drink and stationed himself at the far end of the bar, pretending to have no interest in his environment but his ears tightly attuned to conversations.

The next saloon was not much better. There were more standing at the bar was all, a few more playing cards while above them a stratus of tobacco smoke hung around the lamps.

In the third one he got cornered by some old-timer who wanted to tell him his life story. He knew the type. West or East, you met them everywhere. Bending your ear in the hopes of getting a free drink. He was listening with only half an ear, the bulk of his attention being preoccupied with the matter of his brother's death and what he should do next. Eventually he obliged the oldster with a drink and bade him goodnight.

The fourth establishment, a mite more expensive complete with intact bar-mirror, was more interesting. Not that he heard anything of use. More, a certain face was becoming familiar. A beefy cuss with the dusty garb of a drover. In the last three saloons the fellow had trailed in after him. Johnny went to the bar to buy another drink, using the opportunity to look through the barmirror to get a look at the man. Heavy features, a straw-yellow moustache.

Maybe it was a coincidence. But that could be tested. He threw the drink to the back of his throat and pushed through the batwings into the night air. It was beginning to rain. He thought of Mary and their need for water. He pulled his hat further over his forehead and crossed the street.

He hadn't been in the next saloon

more than a few minutes when the yellow moustache appeared behind him. That clinched it. He took his time with the drink, smoked a cigarette, paying the fellow no obvious interest.

Once more, he left and headed along the boardwalk. Sure enough, he was aware of spurred boots clunking behind him. He used the strategy of crossing the street so that he could throw a sideways look as though checking for traffic as he crossed. His glance was too brief for a detailed examination, but he saw enough to recognize the shape. He continued for some distance along the boardwalk, casually, to give the appearance that he didn't have a care in the world.

Then, still portraying an ambience of indifference, he turned into a narrow alley between two buildings. As he had anticipated, it was dark. Dark enough. Quickly he turned and proned himself against the wall in the first swathe of the blackness near the entrance. A few seconds later, the chink of spurs and a man turned the corner. Johnny grabbed him, whirled him further down the alley. Then gripped his throat and whammed him against the boards.

'Don't shout or even move,' he hissed. 'This is a knife in your gut.'

The man gurgled, his body stiff.

'Now why you tailing me?' Johnny whispered.

'Don't do anything rash, mister,' the man gasped as the grip on his throat relaxed enough for him to speak. 'I'm on your side.'

'What the hell does that mean?'

'There are things you need to know.'

'Is that so? OK, why didn't you approach me in one of the drinking parlours you been following me into?'

'I didn't want to be seen talking to you.'

'Go on.'

'Things ain't right at the Slash S.'

Johnny took his hand from the man and stepped back but kept the knife against the man's belly. 'What's your name?'

'Will. Will Archer. I work for the

outfit. I knew Brendan and Jonas.'

'And?'

'I thought you should know how Brendan really died.'

'Supposed to have been an accident with the cattle.'

'There's accidents and accidents.'

'Well?'

The man looked right and left before continuing. 'The outfit is crook. There's only a handful of straight guys on the payroll. Three Anglos — Brendan, Jonas and me — maybe one or two more and a bunch of Mexes. The three of us, we'd been suspicious for a long time, but we kept our noses clean. What we didn't know wouldn't hurt and we needed our wages. Anyway, it was Jonas who told me about Brendan. Apparently, Brendan had learnt something he shouldn't.'

'Such as what?'

'Manzoni's got his hand in many underhand activities around the territory. He uses the Slash S as a cover. Gun-running, smuggling, rustling over the border. He's a very clever man, keeps his hands clean, operates from a distance. But Brendan had stumbled on Manzoni making a deal with bandits. So he was a witness who could tie in Manzoni directly.'

'Go on.'

'Then some months back, the way Jonas told it, Jonas was out on the range. His horse had thrown a shoe and was unridable. He called one of the drovers and told him what had happened. The guy took his horse and headed back to the remuda to get him a replacement. It would take him maybe an hour, so Jonas moseyed over to a nearby clump of trees, found some shade and took the opportunity for a doze. Says he was woken up by voices. It was Manzoni and a couple of his sidekicks. They hadn't seen Jonas and he was just about to make his presence known when he caught what the boss was saying. Manzoni was talking about Brendan, saying how he needed to be put out of the way. Said they had to make it look like an accident.

'Jonas waited until they'd gone, then headed to the remuda so he could get a horse and warn Brendan himself. But on foot it was two hours before he could get a fresh mount. He knew Brendan was on drag and headed out to his station. When he got there, there was a bit of a commotion. He was told some of the beef had broken away and stampeded. Brendan had been caught up in it and trampled to death.'

'How would they have rigged that?'

'No problem. They either killed him themselves or just knocked him out, then drove cattle over him.'

'And none of you did nothing about it?'

'What could we do? We couldn't confront Manzoni because the same thing would happen to us. And there's no point in telling the law because there's no proof. On top of that, it ain't no secret that Manzoni's got the law sewed up.'

'That explains why Quince is so lackadaisical.' He pondered on the information. 'So my brother *was* killed.'

'Yeah.'

'In that case an account needs paying.' There was cold determination in his voice.

'There's nothing you can do.'

Concluding the guy wouldn't have spoken the way he had unless he was on the level, Johnny stepped back, withdrawing the knife from his belly. He fingered the blade contemplatively before sheathing it. 'Oh, there's a lot I can do.'

'You'll get no help from the law, the sheriff being Manzoni's lackey.'

'I don't need the law.'

'Anyways, when Jonas got shot I figured I'd be next.' The man looked about him again. 'Well now I've got it off my chest I'm litting out.'

'Why?'

The man grunted. 'My first impulse was to light out yesterday as soon as news came through that Jonas had been blown out of his saddle. Things are moving up a peg if they're prepared to gun folk down in the open. Then it occurred to me, if I did vamoose right away, Manzoni would connect the two events and sure as hell send one of his hardcases after me. On the other hand, I figured if I stayed he'd leave it a while before sorting me, otherwise the situation would look real bad. Then I learned about you being Brendan's brother and reckoned you had a right to know. But now I've wised you up on the situation, you might start something. And if you do he'll guess it's connected to me, me being Brendan's pal and all. Then I'll sure end up the same way — and mighty quick. So I've got to disappear now, tonight.'

Johnny shifted a pace along the alley to avoid a drip from a leaky guttering above. 'Where you gonna go?'

'Get the hell out of it, get lost up north somewhere, find a job with another outfit.' He looked at Johnny. 'To be frank I don't see what you can do either. If you ride out to the Slash S making accusations — especially now you've made yourself known as Brendan's brother — you'll get plugged or accidentally end up under cow-hoofs.'

'You're right,' Johnny grunted. 'But as they say out here, there's more than one way to skin a coon.' He mused on the situation. 'Only trouble is, I don't know what Manzoni looks like.'

'Tall feller, about fifty. Always well-dressed.'

'That's a start but it ain't enough. Does he ever come to town?'

'From time to time.'

'What for?'

'Usually to see his crony bigwigs. The sheriff, mayor and judge — they're all in his pocket.'

Johnny nodded. 'Well, back East we have a saying about Mohammed and mountains. And this particular Mohammed has time for the mountain to come to him.'

'Well, whatever you do, you watch your step, pal. And especially your back. Well, so long, pal, and good luck.'

Johnny looked up at the gap of rain-sodden sky between the roofs of the two buildings. 'You got miserable conditions for riding, pal.'

'I can take it. At least litting out at night I'm less likely to be seen.'

'Good luck to you, too. And thanks for being square.'

7

Minutes later he was stamping his wet shoes on the mat in the hotel lobby. He went upstairs. He undressed and got into bed. Blue hell, the wretched thing felt clammy. Worse, mulling over the day's events he couldn't sleep. He tossed and turned. To add to his irritability, he suddenly felt something cold hit the side of his face. He ran his hand over his cheek. It was wet.

He clambered out, lit the oil lamp, and took it over to the bed. There was a steady drip hitting it. He looked up and could see a stain across the ceiling. At its centre there was moisture gathering which fell every few seconds in globules when there was enough weight.

'Hell's teeth,' he mouthed. 'A frigging Niagara.' He considered moving the bed away from the drip but, when he felt the cover and sheets, they were well and truly damp. So that's why it had felt clammy.

Figuring it was too late to rouse the proprietor, he took the lamp out into the corridor and tested doorknobs until he found one unlocked. Casting the light around showed that the room was dry and the ceiling, at the moment, was impervious.

He collected all his gear and moved to his new abode. He found fresh blankets and pillow in the linen cupboard. He made the bed and turned out the lamp. By this time, the invidious downpour had manifested itself as a soft patter against the windowpane with a soothing effect; and he was soon asleep.

★ ★ ★

He was yanked out of his slumber by gunfire. Seconds later he was against the door with gun in hand. He nosed into the corridor. The door to his old room, which he remembered closing, was now open. He ventured towards it. By the time he had inspected it — it was in darkness and empty save for his crumpled covers on the bed — there were other residents in the corridor.

'What's going on?' one asked.

'Your guess is as good as mine.'

The same question was shouted from the end of the passage. It was the proprietor wrapping a dressing-gown round his portly frame and joining the throng.

'Dunno,' Johnny said and returned to his room. He lit the lamp and brought it through. By its light he poked at the wet bed. Moving the sheets he noticed a hole in the side of the mattress. Further investigation revealed two more holes low in the wall on the other side of the bed. He brought out the damp covers and held them up to examine them against the better light of the passage. Eventually he found a couple of rough tears.

'You've not only got running water in this place,' he said, 'you've got running bullets.'

'Who . . . ? The man spluttered. 'What . . . ?'

Johnny ignored the questions and returned to his new room. He jammed a chair against the knob and shifted the bed to the side so it was not in clear view from the door. Once more he lay down, this time with his gun near the pillow. And once more sleep eluded him for some time.

★　★　★

The next morning the sheriff was in the lobby when Johnny came down for his breakfast.

'I told you there's a killing spree going on,' Johnny said. 'Now do you believe me?'

'Well, there was definitely an attempt on your life,' the sheriff said. 'I'll give you that. I've had a look at the room, seen the bullet holes. And a late night reveller in the street tells me he saw a couple of fellows leaving the hotel and riding out about the time. Trouble was it happened so fast and he wasn't in a fit state to see much.'

'And what you gonna do?'

'I understand your concern but, I'm afraid, with no description, ain't much I can do.'

Johnny sat at his regular table. 'I've told you who I reckon is behind it.'

'And I've told you my hands are tied until I have some hard evidence. I can't go round charging folks without facts.' He watched Johnny pour coffee into a china cup. 'More important, what you gonna do?'

Not getting to sleep till the early hours, Johnny had had time to think and was firming up an idea. 'Well, Sheriff, it's clear I'm a target. With you and your 'tied hands' and me with no protection, figure it's best that I just got out of town. Back to quiet old New York.'

'That's the first sensible thing you've said, son.'

'It ain't the *first* sensible thing I've said — and I ain't your son. Now if you'll excuse me I got some coffee to drink and a breakfast to put away. And then some packing to do.'

★   ★   ★

After breakfast he set out for the Blanchard place. He was prepared for the long walk — at least the rain had stopped and the new sun had mopped up surface moisture — then along the way he was lucky enough to hitch a ride from a passing wagon which dropped him close.

Mary Blanchard finished milking. She had just turned the cow out into the poled pasture behind the barn when she saw a figure advancing along the approach track. It was the strange but increasingly familiar garb that she first recognized.

Johnny Doyle.

She returned his waved greeting. He trudged across the yard and slumped onto the step of the veranda. 'This is hotter than New York in a heat-wave,' he said, taking off his hat and rubbing a handkerchief around his brow and neck.

'I'll fetch some lemonade.'

A minute later she put a cold glass in his hand. 'And to what do I owe this honour.'

'Been a busy night, ma'am. First off, a fellow name of Will Archer paid me a visit. A buddy of Brendan's and Jonas. Said Brendan had been killed.'

She sat beside him. 'So your guess was right. It wasn't an accident.'

'An accident — that's what everybody is supposed to think. Appears they trampled his body to make it look like an accident.'

'Who?'

'A couple of Manzoni's men. And they did it on his orders. Just as they put paid to Jonas.'

'But why?'

He related what Archer had told him.

'Have you told the sheriff?'

'No. Now I'm beginning to learn the set-up out here, figure it wouldn't do any good. Manzoni owns the top brass of the town.'

Nonplussed, she shook her head.

'And that ain't the best part,' he said. 'Later in the hotel, a couple of gunnies tried to trigger me.'

Concern showed on her face. 'What happened?'

He went through the scenario.

'This is getting worse,' she gasped when he had finished, her face pale under the tan.

He chuckled humourlessly. 'Worse? That's a good word to describe it.'

'So what you aiming to do?'

'I've had time to think. I got an idea but I'm gonna need some help.'

'Anything I can do, just ask.'

He clenched her hand briefly. 'My biggest problem is Manzoni knows me. He hasn't seen me but he knows that I'm Brendan's brother and will have an idea how I might feel. And there's enough folk have seen me around to have told him what I look like. Last night he demonstrated that he and his gunnies know who I am and what I look like. With Eastern duds and this red hair I stand out like a sore thumb. Already been tagged as the Prince of Wales. Blue hell, can't be many in town who don't know about me by now.'

He glanced to the eastern horizon and, after seemingly studying the terrain, turned back. 'When I first rode in on the stage, there was a town we passed through. Some twenty, thirty miles back maybe. The last stop on the route before Sangrano.'

'Yes, that's Varicaca.'

'You say you'll help?'

'Of course.'

'It won't put you in any danger.'

'What about danger to you? Manzoni is an influential man. What around here they call a big honcho. You think you can take him on by yourself?'

'I've faced toughs before. Besides I've got to do it. At the end of the day a man holds the remedy in his own hands.'

She looked worried. 'Well, if you say so.'

'OK,' he went on. 'I'll make a show of leaving town and catch the stage out to Varicaca. The figure I cut, news will get around that I've gone and Manzoni should hear. Now, I need some Western-style duds. But I don't want to buy new ones, otherwise I'll look like a dude again. They need to be lived-in — and dirtied-up a mite — so I look like some no-account range bum. Can you get me something?'

'You're about the same size as Pa. As luck would have it, there's a load of worn-out stuff in the cupboard. Never throw clothes away. They're useful to cut up into rags.'

He smiled. 'Just the job. The tattier the better.'

'And it'll give me a chance to have a clear out.'

'Don't tell your pa, of course. No need to involve him unnecessarily.'

'No problem.'

He stood up. 'These duds, they include a jacket?' He dropped his hands and touched his sides with his finger-tips. 'I need a fairly long one, finger-length.'

She was puzzled by the sudden precision in his specification but didn't question it. 'No. Only thing like that is Pa's Sunday coat. But I couldn't get that without asking him.'

He shook his head. 'No. Wouldn't do anyhows. It needs to be scruffy, to fit in with the rest of my get-up. Not to worry. I should be able to get one someplace.' He looked to the horizon, his posture reflecting resolution. 'OK. I'll catch the stage and drop off at Varicaca, then walk back a mile or two. You ride out, bringing the duds.' He ran his fingers like a comb through his hair. 'And I need to get this cut off. Must be the only bozo this side of the Pecos with red hair.' His hand fell to his beard and he fingered the strands. 'And nobody knows what I look like under this. So with this off too . . . '

She smiled. 'And I for one would like to know what you look like underneath.

Never did cotton to an unshaved man.'

'I'll need my own transport, too,' he continued, 'so bring Walker, if that's OK. I think the old-timer and I get along well enough together now for me to be able to ride him without an escort.'

★ ★ ★

Early next morning he checked the stage schedule, then walked out to the homestead to let Mary know the departure time and confirm that she was fixed in her part of the operation. Back in town he saw the old Concord creak into town and watched as the vehicle was turned and the team unhitched.

Then he checked out of the hotel, gathered his baggage and went to sit on the bench outside the stage station. He placed his case awkwardly at an angle so passers-by had to walk around it, another ploy to make sure as many townsfolk as possible were aware of his departure.

Eventually a fresh team was put into harness and the Concord was rolled up before the station. Johnny passed his luggage up for it to be positioned on the top rack, then he stepped into the tonneau to join the rest of the passengers.

Shortly the trace-chains were jingling and they were out of town and onto the flats.

A couple of hours on they were rolling into Varicaca. The driver hauled on the brake and the coach came to a standstill, creaking on its leather thorough-braces. Johnny disembarked. He sat on his luggage on the sidewalk and watched the new passengers board. After the coach had left he lit a cigarette and remained seated, deliberately affecting an air of casualness. Then he walked along the town until he saw what he had hoped for — a red-and-white pole.

He picked up his case and walked towards the shingle bearing the title TONSORIAL PARLOR. He stepped inside. For a second the smell reminded him of the last time he had been in a barbershop, but he dismissed the memory and took a seat. Minutes later he was in the barber chair.

He took off his hat and ran his fingers through his long red shanks. 'Fetch this lot off,' he said, trying to put a Western drawl into his speech. 'Damn mop is getting to me in this heat.'

'You want a shaved skull, sir?'

Johnny contemplated for a moment, then judged that that could be attention-grabbing in its own way. 'No. Just cut it right down a mite. Leave, quarter or half an inch, say. And talking about shaving, you can get rid of the whiskers. They're bugging me too.'

When the task was complete, he viewed the effect in the mirror. The flaming red hair was now a stubble. He angled his head this way and that to catch the light in different ways. The violent colour that had once marked his appearance had gone and the remaining bristles were of nondescript hue — could be blond or any fair shade.

Likewise the calling-card fuzz had now been removed from his chin. Mmm, he mused to himself, with a change in clothes he could be a different man.

He paid and returned to the street. With a final glance around the town he headed out into a terrain dotted with prickly pear and brittlebush. Some distance out, the settlement out of view, he espied a tree but yards from the trail. He left the track, noted that the tree provided shade and that the spot gave him a long look along the trail; and he hunkered down to wait. He had a smoke but the heat and soft drone of insects had their effect and, back against the tree, hat over his eyes he drifted off, retrieving some of his lost sleep.

The sound of hoofs rattling along the stony trail brought him back. He opened his eyes to see familiar shapes.

'You look like a road agent in wait up there,' Mary shouted, guiding her horse offtrail and up through the scrub with Walker in tow. 'Nearly missed you. Why didn't you holler?'

'Didn't think you were worth a hold-up,' he chuckled.

He rose and helped her down.

'Got everything you asked for,' she said, opening a saddlebag.

He inspected the garments. The jeans were scuffed, almost threadbare at the knees, with a patch on the thigh. 'Fine. They look lived-in enough. Obliged, ma'am.'

He took off his derby in preparation to change and she laughed.

'What you find funny?' he wanted to know. 'I'm supposed to look like a cowboy not a clown.'

'It's not that. You just look different. Even handsome in a way.'

He grunted a 'Huh', then said: 'Now, if you'll turn around, missy, I'll change.'

She smiled. 'My, the New York man-of-the-world's got some bashfulness too.'

Minutes later he was in shirt and jeans. They were a reasonable fit, but he had some trouble with the boots. 'Ain't never wore long-shanked boots before,' he said, wrestling with the footwear, hauling strenuously at the sides.

'Gonna have to get used to 'em, pardner, if you're aiming to be a cowboy.'

Finally booted, he stood up and tested them, walking awkwardly round in a circle. 'Now I know why cowpokes walk so funny.'

She handed him a wide-brimmed slouch hat with shapeless sides, bearing the stains and scuffs of many years' toil. 'One of Pa's old work hats. He won't miss it.'

He donned it and she laughed again. 'It's not supposed to be perched on the top of your head like that. Pull it down — otherwise it'll blow away in the first puff of wind.'

He did as he was bid and she pulled at the brim, giving it a more rakish angle. 'Now you look like you were born in the saddle.'

He grunted, hobbled ungainly over to Walker and patted the animal on the nose. He put his own gear into the saddlebag, then hurled his valise as far as he could into the brush.

'Mighty big waste of some good leather,' she said.

'Yeah, expensive too. But it's got the look of New York all over it.' He bent down, took some earth and rubbed a little into his face and hands. 'Now when we get back to town, I'm gonna need some lowly place to bunk in,' he said, 'so hotels are out.' He gestured to his clothes and grimed appearance. 'What kind of place in town is appropriate for somebody dressed like this?'

She looked him over. 'There's a drovers' shack to the south of town. Used by passing workers and itinerants.'

'Sounds ideal.'

'I must warn you. I've never been in the place but from its outward looks, I reckon it'll smell a bit.'

'Even better.'

She unfastened the reins of the tow

horse and passed them to him. 'He's all yours.'

He looked at the leathers in his hand and then at the horse. 'And what do I do with him?'

'You ride him, of course. You've learnt that much, haven't you?'

'No — I mean he must eat and drink and stuff. You forget, missy, I ain't familiar with these things.'

She thought on it. 'Tyrone at the livery. He's good with horses. You can quarter him there.'

He mounted up and immediately noted that the high-heeled boots gave him a more secure grip of the stirrups. The strange footwear had one plus at least.

'It's a long ride back,' he said, 'so we'll ride part way together. But nearer town, I'll lay by a spell and you ride in by yourself. Better we aren't seen together.'

'Anything you say — *cowboy*.'

8

He dismounted outside the livery and led horse to the open doorway. An old-timer was sitting by a stove stuffing a pipe with tobacco.

'How much to look after my horse?' Johnny asked.

'Fifty cents a night, feed and water. Forty cents a night thereafter.'

Johnny nodded. 'I was thinking of maybe a week. Resting up before passing on.'

'In that case, mister, paying in advance, figure I could get it down to a flat two dollars.'

'We got a deal. Can you recommend a place for me to rest my back?'

The man crossed the straw-littered floor and looked him over. 'Figure Becky's. It's the drovers' place at the end of the drag.'

Johnny had guessed that would be

the answer but he was playing a stranger in town.

The man chuckled. 'But don't quote me as recommending it. Your hoss is gonna be better accommodated here.'

Johnny grinned as he handed across the reins, and watched the fellow lead Walker to a stall. 'OK,' he said as he left, 'if they got a bunk, that's where I'll be.'

He found the drovers' place where Mary had described it to be. A shack with a couple of chimneys, one straight, one bending like a broken finger. Around the back was a porch on which sat an elderly matron, knitting.

'You got a bed for a traveller, ma'am?' he asked.

She counted on her fingers to conclude: 'Yeah.'

He nodded and she rose to open the door. An unpleasant smell scrambled out, as though grateful to escape, and hit his nostrils. He reconciled himself to the fact that Mary had warned him it would not be as salubrious as his former accommodation. On the other hand he'd smelled worse.

He followed her inside.

'That place is mine,' the woman explained, nodding at a side door as they passed. She took him through and opened the remaining door. There was a single room containing half a dozen beds and nothing else.

'Which one?' he asked after they'd settled the price.

Near them a shape was snoring loudly under blankets. Johnny peered through the unlit gloom and noticed that some article of clothing or travel lay upon each of the other beds as a notice of occupancy, save one. She looked around then pointed at it. 'Seeing's possession is nine points of the law I figure it's that one.'

'That'll do, ma'am.'

'Where's your bedroll?'

'Don't carry such.'

She looked him up and down. 'No bedroll? Strange for a travelling man. Never mind, I got sleeping-gear.'

'Obliged, ma'am.'

'Only two conditions — you pay in advance and you remove your boots.'

He passed over the requisite coin, which she slipped into a purse fixed to her belt. She went into her room and returned with blankets and pillow.

'Folks call me Becky,' she said. 'What do we call you?'

'Wright,' he said. 'Adam Wright.' There was no hesitation. It was the standard reply he gave when cornered by the New York crushers.

'OK, Mr Wright, make yourself to home.'

He crossed to the bed, dropped his saddlebags alongside, laid the pillow and blankets in place and lowered himself onto the cot. He remained still for a while listening to the snoring and snuffling at the other side of the room while he pondered on his next move. He wasn't tired enough to sleep and the night was still young, young enough for him to start his life as Adam Wright, wandering cowpoke.

He dropped the saddlebags on the bed to claim title then walked to the door. He turned on his heel. What was he doing? There was no way he was leaving his belongings unattended in a place like this. He gathered up the bags, turned over the blanket at an angle and left the room.

The woman had resumed her knitting sitting on the porch. 'Everything satisfactory, Mr Wright.'

'Fine, ma'am.'

'Out to discover the pleasures of our little town, are you?'

'Figure, going to bed before nine o'clock would be a dull proceeding, ma'am.'

'Well, have a good time. But any vomiting when you come back, you do it outside.'

'And a good night to you, ma'am.'

⋆ ⋆ ⋆

He knew that his new persona meant he would be restricted to the humbler

108

drinking parlours. He was already familiar with most of the saloons in town and knew that that meant the likes of Logans, his first port of call when he originally arrived in town. He pushed his way through the door. At least a new layer of sawdust had been strewn over the hardened earth of the floor.

He was met by the flat rumble of talk and smell of booze. There was a group gossiping together in a knot by the door. He passed them and went to the bar. When finally served, he took his drink to a table, dumped his bags beside him and watched the goings-on. A group were exchanging jokes at the end of the bar and at the tables there were a couple of card-games in progress.

He watched the play of the nearest game. His only objective was to be seen around, get accepted as part of the scenery. At this point, if he picked up any useful information, that would be a bonus.

He took his drinks slowly. Now and again he would have a smoke and exchange words with someone close.

After an hour he was thinking of moving on when something caught his eye. At one of the cardgames there was an old fellow. Long, grey hair, goatee beard. But what interested Johnny was the guy's jacket. Buckskin, fraying at the edges, grease-stained. Most important, it was long, almost as long as a slicker. It was dangling open so it was difficult to judge exact size. The man was slightly less in stature than Johnny. On the other hand, it was big on the fellow, looking a mite baggy at the shoulders and chest. Even better for Johnny.

He bought himself another drink and wandered over to watch the play. After about half an hour the game was down to two. Finally the oldster threw in a busted flush, his eyes clearly saying goodbye to the last of his money.

His opponent collected his winnings and stood up. 'You got no one to blame but yourself, Billy,' he chuckled. 'I keep telling you — but you do insist on going down to the wire.'

Crestfallen the old man stayed at the empty table for a spell, then staggered over to the bar. He squeezed a ring from his finger and held it up. 'How much you give me for that, Ned?'

The barkeep held out his hands revealing a motley of rings on both. 'What would I do with another ring, Billy?'

'You could sell it.'

'Billy, I keep telling you, I ain't running a hock business. You must be deaf in your old age. You try this caper at least once a week. And you get the same flea in your ear.'

Johnny went to the bar and leant on the beer-swilled surface close to the old-timer. 'I'll buy you a drink, feller,' he said.

'You will?'

'On one condition.'

'What's that?'

'You play me cards using your jacket as the stake.'

A quizzical expression distorted the man's features and he looked down at the garment. 'This old thing?'

'Yeah. Just right for me out on the trail.'

'How much is it good for?' the old man said, his voice changing to cockiness with the notion that he had an asset desirable to a second party. He stuck his thumbs in the lapels and examined it as though to make a rational appraisal.

Johnny shrugged. 'How much *you* reckon it's worth?'

'Figure I could get four dollars for it, mister.'

Johnny chuckled. 'More like two, you old hornswoggler. But I'll go along with staking you for four.'

'You will? You're on, mister.'

Johnny gestured to the barkeep. 'And whatever the gentleman is drinking.'

A drink was poured, of which the old-timer quaffed half before he'd left the bar to join his new benefactor.

Johnny took up position at the table

and put four coins before him. 'There's my four dollars,' he said as the man made to sit down. 'Now you put your stake on the table.'

'What's that?'

'The jacket. Remember?'

With an 'Oh, yeah' the befuddled oldster cleared the pockets from the garment, then laid it on the table.

'Draw poker,' Johnny said. 'Best of a single deal, and you can deal.'

'Anything you say, boss,' the other said and began shuffling.

At the end of the deal, Johnny laid his cards exposed on the table. The best he had was two fours. The old man chuckled. Johnny asked for two, his opponent drew three. The man stopped chuckling when he saw that Johnny now had three fours against his own two queens.

Johnny leant over and placed his hand on the jacket. 'OK?' he said, as though asking permission to take his winnings.

'OK,' the other grunted, 'but I sure

don't enjoy losing to a stranger.'

'You're right to feel that way, pal,' Johnny said. He hefted the garment in his hand as though making his own valuation. 'You know, pal, I reckon this cost ten dollars new.' He laid it across the saddlebags at his side. He took coins from his pocket and counted six in front of the old man, then pushed his original stake of four across the table. 'By my figuring that's ten. Fair exchange?'

The man's eyebrows rose, then he grabbed the money as if claiming his good fortune before the sky fell in.

'Night,' Johnny said, picking up his saddlebags with the jacket over them.

The man didn't answer. Clutching the coins, he was staggering to the bar as Johnny left.

In the street Johnny headed for the drovers'. He'd won the hand purely on luck. He'd shuffled pasteboards in speakeasies since he was ten and, if he had played the deck for a few hands back there in Logans and learned something of the lay of the cards, there was ample sleight in his fingers to have ensured a win. But he also had enough sense to know he was a stranger and didn't know how many friends the old man had in the place. Which is why he also showered the codger with dollars as a finale, so there would be no grudges — and no one to charge him with grifting a local oldster in his cups.

OK, he had drawn some attention to himself, but that couldn't be avoided. Might even be to his advantage, giving him a new image, helping him to blend in with the town. But it was of no consequence. For a measly ten dollars he had exactly what he wanted.

Back at the drovers', Miss Becky's head poked out from her door as he passed.

'Hope I didn't disturb you, ma'am,' he said as he passed.

'No, ain't gone to bed yet. Just checking who it was is all.'

'As you're still about, you got a length of string or something I could have? I need to tie a bundle.'

She opened the door and he could see her rummaging through a drawer. Eventually she came up with a thin sliver of rawhide. 'That do, young man?'

'Fine. Thanks. 'Night, Miss Becky.'

In the bunkroom, he tried on the jacket. It was a little slack on his frame but that was to its advantage. And the length was more than ample.

Seated on his cot, he rolled up the garment and put it into one of the saddlebags. He tied the end of the rawhide to the crosspiece of the bags and pushed the gear under his bed. He got into bed and tied the end of the rawhide to his wrist before pulling up the blanket.

As he lay in the darkness he heard others returning to the accompaniment of grunting and the breaking of wind. Then followed the whisper of oaths as toes stubbed unseen objects in the dark. He turned over and, against a symphony of belching, the rip of unbuttoning, the sound of palliasses creaking, he finally went to sleep.

9

Two days on a stroke of luck came his way. He was walking past the Constitution Hotel. The building commanded the finest prospect in town, two storeys with mock Grecian wooden pillars at the front. And he'd noted that it was being bedecked with coloured bunting.

'What's the occasion?' he asked a local loading up a wagon outside a dry-goods store. 'By my reckoning July Fourth has passed.'

'Elections,' came the reply. 'Mayor, sheriff, judge, the whole caboodle.'

Feigning interest, Johnny cast his eyes up and down the edifice. 'Mighty impressive.'

'I should say so. Wouldn't expect a lesser show from Manzoni.'

Now he *was* interested. 'Manzoni?'

'Yeah, that fuss is all in celebration of the election of his candidates.'

'When are the elections?'

'Booths are open now. Close at nine tonight.'

'But how does this Manzoni know that his candidates will win?'

The old man chuckled, pausing in his task to give Johnny the once-over. 'You sure are a stranger in town. Same every year. Manzoni's boys get re-elected whatever the outcome.' He lowered his voice and looked around. 'God knows what happens to the real voting papers. So much for democracy. There'll come a time when these things are done proper — if ever Arizona becomes a state — but in the meantime . . . '

Johnny nodded. It was in the same way that the gangs had sewn up Tammany Hall back in New York. The more he heard about this place the more it was becoming a home from home.

Johnny picked up a sack of meal from the sidewalk. 'Here, let me give you a hand.' Then, 'This Manzoni fellow, does he come to the celebrating?'

'Sure does. One of the few times he honours the town with his presence.'

Now a chance to see what the critter looked like! 'What time does the celebration start?'

'Nine o'clock. Soon as polls close.'

'And who's invited?'

'The whole town. Free food and liquor. Manzoni's way of keeping in with the townsfolk. It works.'

* * *

At the stipulated time that evening Johnny, with grime washed from his face and hands, mixed in with the throngs approaching the Constitution Hotel. Now hung with Chinese lanterns, the frontage was even more resplendent.

There was a bull-ox of a man standing at the door. He wore a creased evening jacket but it didn't hide the range-gear he wore underneath. He had a thick neck and the unpleasant features of inbreeds that Johnny had seen in the worst areas of the East Side. There are some folks you could dress in the most expensive clothes, Johnny mused, and they would still look a cretin — and this bozo was one of them. As people entered the fellow nodded and cracked his face in an attempt at a smile. But the smile was more like the leer of some demon from a nightmare.

A couple of young sports in Sunday best with starched shirts ambled along the sidewalk and laughed in good spirits as they passed the bouncer. Johnny dropped in step behind them but was stopped by a huge hand on his shoulder. 'Whoa there, young feller. No saddle bums.'

It was the ox.

'I didn't think invitations were necessary,' Johnny protested.

'They ain't. But this shindig is for the good people of the town, not wandering saddlebums. Now git.'

Johnny walked away, now realizing that his disguise, so useful up to now, had certain drawbacks. Back at the drovers' he had another wash, then donned some of his Eastern clothes: shirt, trousers, shoes. Then, minus hat, he returned to the Constitution. The same bouncer was on the door but this time Johnny kept his distance, satisfying himself for the time being with just watching the visitors enter.

After a while a matronly-looking woman and what looked like her daughter passed him on the boardwalk. The refinement of their dresses broadcast they were heading for the festivities.

He sprang smartly behind them. 'Are you two ladies going to the celebration?'

The elder lady turned to look him up and down askance. 'Why, yes, young man,' she replied hesitantly.

'Then allow me the honour to escort you inside.'

They giggled at each other as he wormed his way between them and took their arms. He chatted with them about the mildness of the evening as they approached, switching to commenting on the attractiveness of the

Chinese lanterns as they passed the bouncer without question.

Inside, tables had been pushed together to provide a continuous buffet while waiters worked their way through the crowd with trays of cocktails and canapés. At the side a couple of fiddlers and a pianist played 'Bringing Out The Sheaves'. Johnny noticed a punchbowl at the end of one of the tables. He gestured in its direction. 'Punch, ladies?'

'Why that's very kind, young man.'

'Then allow me to be your waiter.'

A minute later, he was handing them full glasses. 'Enjoy the evening, ladies,' he said with a bow. And with that he returned to the punchbowl and poured himself a glass to serve as a prop.

From then on he stood taciturnly on the side-lines, watching and listening. The crowd consisted of town dignitaries and tradesfolk decked in their finest, with a fair sprinkling of stand-up collars and patent leather shoes. There was a makeshift stage at the back covered in flowers and bunting. Still keeping near the wall, Johnny edged nearer.

Some time in, he noted Mary and her father amongst the milling crowds. She caught his eye and began to move in his direction but he shook his head. She recognized his signal and veered from her course to stop and talk to someone else.

Getting nearer the stage he saw three men leaning against the boards. Concerned with their own conversation, they took no part in the socializing. They looked different from the rest too, dressed in range gear with guns on their hips. There was every chance these were some of Manzoni's men.

He mixed into the edge of the crowd and moved closer to the gunnies. Listening and occasionally looking their way he managed to pick up a couple of names. One who had jagged teeth that protruded through thin red lips, giving him a weasel appearance went by the name of Abilene. Hatch was another — a short, stubby man with greying hair cropped Teutonic style. One spoke with authority, suggesting he was the leader of the little coterie. He was six foot of slack muscle, slouching against the stage, thumbs hooked in his gunbelt, but Johnny couldn't catch his name.

Suddenly the sloucher said, 'Stand by. Boss's here.'

Johnny looked across and saw a group of quality-dressed men gathering in preparation to mount the stage on the far side and there was a clatter at the front of the building denoting the closing of the entrance doors.

The group crossed the stage and took up occupancy in chairs behind a table. One rose and banged the table. 'Ladies and gentlemen, your attention please. The counting of the votes is almost complete. But before the results are announced I have invited local businessman and major town benefactor, Mr Monte Manzoni, to say a few words. So please give a hearty Sangrano welcome to our chief guest.'

He stepped back and a tall figure stepped forward, bedecked in ruffled shirt, mauve cravat with a jewelled pin. Johnny studied his features. Maybe fifties. Large ears, trim silver moustache, with a shallow complexion that hinted that he conducted his octopus machinations behind closed doors away from the Arizonan sun.

So this was the bastard who murdered from a distance.

'Ladies and gentleman . . . ' the man began. But that was all Johnny heard. Suddenly out of nowhere the bull-ox from the front door was squeezing past. Johnny turned his head but the fellow caught sight of his face. 'Hey, you're the bum I said couldn't come in.'

'What me? No, pal. Must be somebody else.'

The ox looked him up and down. 'You've changed your duds — but you're still a bum. You're going out.'

By the beefy hands reaching out to him, Johnny figured it had been a long time since the guy had practised

Scarlatti after lunch. However, unrefined as the mitts were, they were amply suitable for the task in hand and before Johnny could do anything, he was in a vice-grip being frog-marched to a side door. Out in the darkness of the alley, one of the ham fists smashed into Johnny's midriff. 'I don't cotton to somebody treating me like a mug,' the ox growled. 'Understand?'

Johnny did not want to be the focus of anything. It was bad enough, the start of the confrontation being witnessed by bystanders in the hall, and he didn't want to draw any more attention to himself; at that point he should have accepted the admonition and left. But the New Yorker had got a temper; and this pea-brained inbred had whammed him painfully in the gut. The guy was far bigger than he, but Johnny had the advantage of surviving in East Side backstreets. And he went into automatic drive. His knee jerked up into the man's crotch. As his head came forward, Johnny's flattened palms scythed into the soft flesh on either side of the man's neck just above the chest bone. The fellow dropped to his knees and Johnny swung his right hand back to chop the man in the throat — when rationality suddenly reasserted itself and he stopped himself just in time. There was every chance it would have been a killing blow — it had happened before — and his brain told him he had done enough damage already.

Semi-conscious, the ox slumped face down in the soil of the alley as Johnny nipped back to enter the street. He'd hoped to hang around longer and possibly see which way Manzoni left, maybe even retrieve the faithful Walker from the livery stable and follow him. But putting paid to the bouncer had ruled out that course of action.

On the way back to his drovers' bunk, he summarized the evening. At least he had learned what Manzoni looked like.

10

The days passed with no new developments and he was becoming increasingly frustrated. He had to find a way of learning the location of Manzoni's base. He knew the man came to town occasionally but, thanks to his temper, the waiting on the off-chance could now mean a long wait. If he hadn't downed that ox in the alley he could have hung around without arousing suspicions or animosity and possibly have seen Manzoni leave. No use crying over spilt . . .

Then one evening a new resident took up occupancy at Becky's. There was always a steady turnover of clients but most kept themselves to themselves. This one was a puncher travelling between jobs, staying over for one night. He came in late and was allocated the adjacent bunk as Johnny was preparing to go out.

'Name of Earl,' he said, thrusting out a solid working hand. 'Folks just call me Earl.' They exchanged a few words then the man said, 'What about the two of us palling up for the night? See the town. Be company for each other.'

Johnny agreed and they trawled the saloons. But the man couldn't handle his ale and there came a point when Johnny wanted to cut himself off from his new-found company. The man was wasting his time and damn boring to boot. He should have known. A guy looking for a drinking partner usually had problems.

Eventually they ended up in one of the more respectable-looking establishments. But with the steady flow of couples up and down the stairs, Johnny didn't have to be a Pinkerton detective to know it was brothel.

The puncher eyed the girls drunkenly, bending his head in an attempt to look up their dresses as they mounted the stairs and whispering ribald comments to his companion.

Then: 'How long you in town for?' he asked.

Johnny shrugged. 'Dunno, maybe another week.'

'I tell you where I'd be if I was staying over longer and hadn't come in so damn late.'

'Where's that?'

'Old Man Heeley's. Trouble is, it's way out of town.' He giggled. 'See, he's got this daughter and he lets you have her for two dollars.' He chuckled. 'Even less if you're broke. She'll let you do anything.' He twirled his finger round the side of his head. 'Mind, she's a bit, you know. So's her father, come to that. But at those prices, who cares? Cheap booze too, home-made stuff.' He waved around the room. 'Not these fancy prices. Yes, sir, that's where I'd be if I had the time. Spent some real pleasurable evenings there.'

'A saloon — out in the sticks?'

'No, it ain't a saloon. A soddy just off

the trail. Kind of store for passing traffic. Got bits and pieces for repairs to wheels, saddles and stuff. Shoes horses too, got a smithy round the back. The home-made booze and the girl, they're just his way of earning something extra.'

Johnny nodded, not really interested.

'So,' the other went on, 'you being in town a spell, you should give it a whirl. You'll have a good time, and it won't cost you much at all. Fact is, can't think of a cheaper night's funning anyplace, anywheres. And I been around, pal.'

'Could try it,' Johnny said out of politeness with no intention of following it up. 'Thanks for the notion.'

'Well, here's how you get there.' The man gave directions which Johnny didn't absorb. 'Can't miss, it,' he concluded. 'Right out on the edge of the Slash S spread.'

Johnny's ears pricked up.

'That reminds me,' the man mumbled into his beer. 'That's the only problem.'

'What do you mean?'

'Well, being on the edge of the Slash S, their boys take it over some nights. Ain't worth any outsider staying when they move in. The bozos see it as their private club. Cheap booze and taking it turns wing-dinging the gal.'

Johnny's interest was kindled. There was little to be gained from returning to the ranch headquarters but at this Heeley's place he might be able to learn something. And it might prove more profitable than just hanging around town.

'How did you say I get there?' he asked.

★ ★ ★

The next night Johnny rode out and eventually found the store. It was a crudely built shack about fifty yards off the trail. He reined in some distance away and tethered his horse to some scrub. Approaching on foot, he soon assessed the place to be in complete darkness. Closer, he could see a hitch rail but no horses. With nothing to be pursued that night he crept back to his mount and returned to town.

The following night was different. Even from the trail this time he could see light poking from gaps between curtains. And there were horses at the rail. He tethered Walker in the same place as the previous night and made his way to the building.

He raised the latch and entered. The room was smelled up with the rank odour of flat, home-made beer and rotgut whiskey. At the back with elbows resting on the counter, sat an elderly man, brown overall hanging open. Johnny figured that had to be Heeley. Eyes sagging, the fellow looked like he was ready for bed — but would still be available as long as anyone was still willing to pay.

And there were three drinkers who were clearly still willing to pay. All turned to look at the newcomer and he recognized them as the trio from the shindig at the Constitution Hotel.

'Private party, mister.' The speaker was leaning against the bar, the slack-muscled sloucher whom he had pegged as a boss. 'So make yourself scarce pronto.' He turned back to the shot glass of whiskey before him.

Johnny took stock of the others. Near him there was the short man with Teutonic hair-style. Well apart from them, the third, the thin red-lipped weasel.

Johnny had indeed intended taking a drink but now that it had been made clear that that option was not available, he decided to take a chance, see what happened. 'Ain't looking for refreshment,' he said. 'Just want a piece of information, is all.'

'I don't think you heard me arights,' the slouch at the bar said without turning. 'This place ain't available to you for refreshment or information.'

'Now that puzzles me,' Johnny said. 'See, it's my understanding you can oblige me. Mind, I ain't looking for trouble.'

'Then what are you looking for? Entertainment? We can give you that. We're in need of some entertainment too, ain't we, boys?'

Drunken affirmation was voiced around the room.

'No,' the New Yorker pressed, 'just want to know where Monte Manzoni lives.'

The man at the bar sank the shot of whiskey — as though in preparation for something — and turned. 'You ain't learning nothing here, pal.' He waved a hand at the others, 'Abilene, cover him. Hatch, you frisk him.'

Guns came out quickly as the weasel dashed over to him. Up close, the fellow gusted foul-smelling breath into the New Yorker's nostrils. The scrawny fingers wormed up and down his sides, round his legs, patted his backside. 'Clean, boss.'

By now the slouch was some steps nearer. 'Why-for you want to know about Mr Manzoni?'

'Business.'

The man grunted. 'Business? Well, like I said, this ain't no information bureau. But we can sure give you some entertainment. Hold him, boys.'

Before Johnny could do anything he was gripped on either side. Slouch delivered a fast one-two combination. The first went to the stomach bringing Johnny's head forward, the second to the jaw, whipping back the victim's head. Another to the stomach and Johnny's legs went. His restrainers guffawed and let him slump to his knees.

But it wasn't the first time Johnny had been at the hard end of fists. Which was why he knew, despite being outnumbered, he had some advantages. For a start, the more you've taken, the less you get fazed by the infliction of pain; and the more you can take. Plus, his attackers had all imbibed some liquor, taking the edge off their capability. Contrariwise his head — as long as they didn't kick the shit out of it — was still clear.

He lay still for a moment. While prepared for further blows, he guessed — rightly — they were gloating on their success and assessing what state he was in.

Then he let them know what state he was in. His left fist shot sidewards, straight into the balls of the weasel while his boot heel crashed into the ankle of Close-Crop bringing him down. Launching forward he shouldered into the Slouch's stomach, slamming him against a table.

'You're wrong,' Johnny hissed, moving forward to wham another into the man's jaw before he recovered. 'I have learned something. There's more rotten little jerks out here than in all the shittiest tenements on the East Side put together.'

He'd just crunched knuckles into the man's face again when the inside of his head exploded in a vortex of spiky lights as something crashed into the side of it — and he went down again. The slouch wiped his lips with the back of his hand, inspected the blood and shambled forward.

'Shit? We'll show you shit.' He bent over and yanked Johnny to his feet, ramming him against the wall, then fisted him in the face. As Johnny slithered down the woodwork, the fellow brought up his knee. Johnny sensed his teeth smashing together and he could taste blood.

As he keeled awkwardly over to the floor, a hard boot lashed into his cheek, jerking back his head yet again.

He squinted through slitted eyes to see the boot of the weasel going back for another kick. He was thinking how the hell he could avoid it when the chief pulled the weasel back. 'No more, Abilene. He's in bad shape. Any more and we'll as like kill him. Mr Manzoni's got enough troubles without another dollop. Pity, I was enjoying it. Anyways, figure the critter's learnt his lesson. Hatch, show him the door.'

Johnny felt hands grab him and he was hurled across the room to land in a heap at the foot of the door.

'When you can stand, get back to whatever hole you crawled out of,' the slouch said and returned to the bar. 'Reckon this calls for another drink, Heeley.'

At this juncture the back door crashed open and a man was pulling on his pants. 'What the hell's the racket?' Behind him stood a young girl in a tattered chemise. 'Can't a man have a quiet frig in peace?' he boomed.

'You're too late, Lando,' one said. 'You've missed the fun.'

Johnny recognized the bull-ox who had evicted him from the Constitution. But he could tell there was no recollection in the man's eyes. The swaying of the head on the thick neck and the difficulty the man had in focusing suggested the amount of liquor he had imbibed might give him trouble in identifying even his mother.

Johnny lay still for a moment, pulling together whatever resources he had left. He hauled himself slowly to his feet to stand unsteadily with the look of a man who had lost battle and cause. Remarkably his hat was still on his head, albeit at a crazy angle, but as he rubbed his hands over his face he dislodged it completely.

The big Lando was still looking at him and a flicker of recognition showed in his eyes now the hat had fallen away, giving him a clear view of Johnny's face and the hatless scalp he had seen at the Constitution.

'You,' he snarled. 'I know you.' He looked back at his *compadres*. 'It was *him* at the shindig,' he said jerking a thumb back at Johnny. 'The one I threw out.'

'The one who put your lights out?' one of the others sniggered. 'That pipsqueak? You're sure losing your touch, big man.'

'Right,' the ox bellowed and began to lumber towards the visitor. 'I'm settling your hash for good and all.'

'Hold it, Lando,' the slouch shouted. 'If he's the same feller, maybe there's more to this than we figured. We'd best rope him up and tell Manzoni. Maybe he'll want to question the bozo.'

'Question the bozo? I'll question him. I'm gonna frigging kill him.'

The pause was enough for Johnny. There was a sudden blur of movement — and there was a gun in his hand! And not just any gun. One that would not look out of place mounted between two wheels and being trundled round a battlefield.

The first shot from the colossus punched a crater in the chest of the approaching Lando and he fell, thudding to the boards like the ox he was. The others went for their guns. But the weasel spun like a top, blood gushing from the main artery in his neck, the bullet from his own gun thunking into the rafters above. The slouch was blasted against the counter and bounced forward, groping at the torn flesh of his belly as he hit the planking.

Johnny's final bullet took away a large hunk of bone from the close-cropped skull of the Teuton and he crumpled to the floor to lie as still as only a dead thing could be.

A blueness tinged the atmosphere of the whole room; and the previous liquor-stink was now obliterated by the smell of burnt powder.

The barkeep was against the shelves, hands raised and whimpering, 'Nothing to do with me, pal.'

'Come out,' Johnny said.

The man obliged while Johnny scoured the back of the bar, found a Winchester and shucked the shells from it. 'Just in case you're tempted,' he said. 'Now get me a bottle of whiskey and a glass. Then sit over there where I can see you.'

Shortly he was sitting at a table, bottle and glass before him, the gun close at hand. He poured whiskey over his head. He took out a handkerchief and, wincing, patted the damp cloth over his cuts and bruises. The girl from the back, thirteen, maybe fourteen years of age, stood looking at him.

Meanwhile the storekeeper's gaze had fallen to the gun. Like a cannon. Barrel at least eight inches long. And 50 calibre by the damage it had done to the paltry flesh and bones of his customers. Where the hell had it come from? The guy hadn't come in with a gun — and they'd frisked him!

Johnny finally sloshed whiskey into the glass and took a full mouthful, sloshing it around his mouth. He ejected the lot in a red stream onto the boards and gingerly felt around his jaw. Bastards had loosened some of his teeth.

He took a sip of the whiskey and savoured it sliding down his throat as he surveyed the still, bloody battlefield. 'Well they did say they wanted some *entertainment*.' He looked back at the proprietor. 'These critters come here a lot, don't they? Or at least *did*. Over a long time.'

'Yes.'

'Their boss, this Manzoni, he come too?'

'From time to time.'

'So you know him.'

'I'm acquainted with him.' Eager to placate, he pointed to the girl. 'Listen, mister, you want the girl? You can have one, no charge.'

Johnny shook his head. 'So you know where I can find Manzoni?'

'No, sir. Don't know him that well.'

'Listen, you can tell by our silent audience here that I don't cotton to being messed with. This being a private drinking-parlour, them being in their cups, loosing off their mouths, and you being behind that bar — you couldn't avoid picking up all kinds of things. Now I ain't a mug. I *know* you know — or you have a pretty good idea — so stop fiddle-footing.'

The man squirmed. 'Listen, mister, it'd be more than my life's worth. You don't know what Manzoni is capable of.'

'I *do* know. And *you* know what *I'm* capable of.' To make his point he gestured to the nearest corpse — the

144

crop-haired heavy whose life-blood had subsequently pumped from his head to obliterate the Teutonic features.

Then, he took another sip of his drink. 'Listen, these are stiffs,' he said in an almost confidential tone. 'They ain't gonna argue. If Manzoni comes to learn that I've found out where he holes up and he challenges you, you can tell him one of these bozos told me,' — he pointed the long barrel upwards — 'before they went to see their maker.'

The man squirmed some more. 'Can I have a drink? I don't normally drink but I sure need one.'

'Feel free. It's your place. But I'm watching you.'

The man claimed a glass from behind the bar, returned and topped it up from the bottle.

'You know Tucson?' he asked after he had slung it back in one go.

'Know of it but ain't never been.'

'Well, he's got a place out there. See, he's got business interests all over the territory. Fingers in many pies. The

Slash S outfit is only one. His residence in Tucson is his main base.'

'So where exactly is his place?'

'That's all I know, mister.'

Johnny rose. 'You'd better be telling me the truth, friend.' He waved the gun in the direction of the man who closed his eyes and crossed himself muttering, 'On Mother Mary.'

'Oh, you're a Roman, too?' Johnny said.

'Yes, sir.'

Johnny retrieved his hat, donned it with one hand while keeping his gun in the other. He nodded to the girl. 'Well, next time at confession tell Father what you're doing to your gal there.'

'Say, mister,' Heeley said. 'Mr Manzoni's gonna be asking me a heap of questions about all this. What do I say?'

'Tell him what you like.' Now his temper had brought something of his cause into the open there was no point being coy. 'Tell him what you saw.' He crossed to the door.

'You've put me in hell of a spot,

mister,' the man whined. 'He'll want to know the whys and where-fores.'

Johnny opened the door and looked back. 'Tell him it's payback time.'

'Payback time?'

'Yeah. If he doesn't understand right away, it should dawn on him.'

'And who shall I say?'

Johnny ignored the question, made to leave but reflected and paused. Even though his mouth hurt he smiled. He was beginning to enjoy his little game. 'Tell him — the Expediter.'

Outside he sensed the coolness of the night air and, enjoying a modicum of rejuvenation, drew it deep into his lungs.

He returned to his horse and hunkered down to watch the building. He figured it wasn't yet midnight so there was lots of time. There was a chance the proprietor had given him the wrong information. Plus a chance he would light out to Manzoni to tell him what had happened. If so, Johnny could follow him.

At first he refused to acknowledge his fatigue. He mused on the night's events. He had hoped that merely hanging around he might have learned more about Manzoni. But when that avenue had been blocked from the moment he had walked into the place, his innate impetuosity and to-hell-with-the-consequences attitude had taken over once again and he'd had the crazy notion he could goad the Manzoni men into revealing something. He knew he would probably have to take some hard knocks. It had been a mite rougher than he'd anticipated but there was always something that could be salvaged. And from this? If the guy back there wasn't lying, he had learned his time would be more profitably spent combing Tucson. Plus, he estimated he had removed a good proportion of the opposition. And some icing on the cake: the enjoyment of knowing that when Manzoni heard — he would be shit-scared.

But half an hour on, there was no activity from the building and the ordeal of the night was making itself known on his body with a vengeance, reminding him he needed to rest, to restore energy for the ride to Tucson. As it was, it had been a busy and not unprofitable night. He heaved himself into the saddle and headed back to town.

11

'The Expediter? Who the frigging hell's the Expediter?'

'Don't know, boss. That's all he said.'

Manzoni went to the door. 'Piker, Caleb. Come and listen to this.'

A minute later the two henchmen had joined them. After Manzoni had acquainted them with the news he turned back to Heeley. 'And what's this about payback?'

'He said you'd know.'

'Like hell I do.' He mused on the situation. 'Payback? It's got me beat. Well, you're the only one left standing so what can you tell me about him?'

'Nothing to tell. It all happened so fast. Only thing I know he talked like a dude.'

'What do you mean — a dude?'

'Like a banker or something.'

Manzoni contemplated some more.

'How the hell does a dude wipe out four of my best men?'

'He can handle a gun, I'll tell you that.'

'Now that's what you might call insight,' Manzoni grunted cynically. 'Insight? It's frigging obvious, you bozo.' He thought on it. 'What do you mean — like a banker? Was he dressed like a banker?'

'No, regular range clothes. In fact, worse than that. Looked more like a saddle bum.'

'So what's this about he talks like a dude?'

'Funny, you know. Talked like he's a Yankee or comes from the East or something.'

Manzoni gave another grunt. 'I tell you one thing: the more *you* talk the less I understand.' He crossed the room and leant on the mantel. 'Was he big, fat, or what?'

'I'm just trying to think.'

'You in-breeds get me. Did he have horns, a tail, breathe fire?'

Heeley held out a flattened palm at

head level, moving it up and down, staring at it as he tried to recall the stature. 'Average height, a mite less maybe. He doesn't carry much weight but he's got a body that can take punishment. I've seen men go down from a lot less.'

'And where did the gun come from?'

'Dunno. Abilene frisked him when he first showed up. Clean.'

'A gun out of thin air? So he's magic as well, eh? What kind of shooter was it?'

'Big job. Never seed anything like it. First slug threw Lando back about six feet. You can judge for yourself when you see the holes it made. More like a cannon than a regular sidearm.'

'You sure you weren't drinking?'

Heeley shook his head. 'The bodies need moving, boss. They're beginning to stink up the place.'

'Stink up the place?' Manzoni queried. He laughed. 'Your place?'

'I mean — shall I tell the funeral parlour?'

'No. I'll send one of the boys across just to look it over. Maybe he can learn something. He'll tell the coffin man.' He slumped into a huge leather chair and lit a cigar. 'Any idea what it was all about? Did it start off with the boys joshing him for fun or what?'

Heeley remained quiet.

Manzoni growled. 'Listen, Heeley. I can tell there's something you ain't telling me.' He banged the floor with his heel. 'You're as thick as these planks. There's only one thing you know and that's brewing liquor. It's all you in-breeds over there can do. That's why the only option for you is to make cents by poisoning the brains of passers-by with your hooch — while your gal poisons their peckers. What is it? You can't hide anything from me.'

'This feller knows your main residence is in Tucson,' Heeley blurted.

'How the hell does he know that?'

'Abilene told him.'

'Abilene wouldn't do that.'

'He was at the mercy of this guy. It

was with his last breath and this guy, a real mean critter, was making it worse for him.' His voice lowered. 'And there's something else I've just remembered. Lando had seen him before. Said he'd thrown him out of that shindig you held for the mayor and such.'

Manzoni thought. 'Heard there was a bit of trouble. Didn't pay it no mind at the time.' He thought on it some more and his face tightened. 'But if the bozo was there at the Constitution it means he knows what *I* look like.'

He looked at the other. 'Let me get this straight,' he said sternly 'There's a crazy galoot out there with some grudge against me. He's killed a passel of my best men. He knows what I look like. And he knows where I live.'

'That's the size of it.'

Manzoni drew heavily on his cigar and blew out smoke through gritted teeth. 'You know, in Roman days, when somebody brought a passel of bad news to the emperor, the emperor used to have the messenger disembowelled.'

'Don't know about that, Mr Manzoni. What's it mean? Dis-, dis- . . . ?'

'It means, I think you'd better vamoose before I remember that my folks being Italian means I've got Roman blood running through my veins.'

When Heeley had left, Manzoni looked at his sidekicks. 'Right. Get word out to Roscoe over in Benson. Tell him I got a job for him. Then you two find out who this critter is. We know he's around five seven, five eight tall. Short hair. Dressed like a grubliner with a long buckskin jacket, black hat. Got a Yankee accent. More important, find out where he's at. If he doesn't know *exactly* where I live in Tucson he'll still be scouting around town. We have enough friends in town for somebody to finger a stranger asking after me. Plus, with the description we've got, we should soon find out where he's staying. When you find out where, give Roscoe the details.'

★ ★ ★

It was a long ride. The severest test so far of his newly acquired riding skills. Following his established pattern Johnny had found accommodation in a drovers' put-up. Only difference from Sangrano, this one in Tucson was adobe like most of the other buildings in town. Just off the Calle Real, the town's main thoroughfare, it gave him easy access to the saloons where he did his questioning.

* * *

The man riding past the old Presidio into Tucson had an enigmatic slant to his eyes and prominent cheekbones that suggested some Indian heritage. The fading poncho added to the suggestion. But an Indian was unlikely to sport the well-kept six-guns that sat in the oiled holsters under the poncho.

Roscoe Styles applied his mind to the job in hand. The description he had been given was distinctive enough so he'd got an idea of what his victim looked like and where he was bunked up. But first he needed to familiarize himself with the layout of the place, which he did by riding up the Calle Real, noting the intersections. Then to get close to the man to make sure he had the right target. It was no never-mind to him that he might kill the wrong man along the way before achieving a successful completion to his task; it was killing somebody without getting paid for it that he didn't cotton to.

He had a couple of advantages. The guy didn't know what *he* looked like or that he was gunning for him. As with many towns in the locality the sheriff was in Manzoni's pocket so when the lead started flying he wouldn't have to concern himself with the law nosing in.

Manzoni's contacts had located the man bunking in a drovers' in a side street. When Roscoe had committed the geography to memory he ambled down the side-street, found the drovers'. He dropped into a chair outside a cantina opposite the place, to watch and wait.

He took a pack of cornshuck papers from his vest pocket and tapped tobacco into one. He lit up and leant back, content to take his time. Several men came and went but none fitted the description. A couple of cigarettes later a figure emerged, black slouch hat, long scuffed buckskin jacket. Had all the makings of the grubline drifter he was after. He flicked away the cigarette butt and fell in step.

The sun was reaching its zenith as he followed the man onto the Calle Real and past the main plaza. He paused when he saw the man turn and enter a door under a shingle marked *EATS*. He leant on a rail for a few moments, pretending to watch the passing traffic, then entered the eating-house.

His quarry had taken up a seat near the kitchen door at the rear. Roscoe dropped into a seat near the front window. His eyes and ears were shrewd in their inspection. The man had asked what was on the menu and it was plain he was not of local stock. Not only was there no West in his mode of speech but the waiter's response of *frijoles* and *tortillas* had to be explained to him. By the time the man had settled on the offering together with a helping of the more familiar roast beef, Roscoe had pinpointed the voice to New York. This was his man all right.

He took a quick coffee to excuse his presence then left. Outside he took in the Calle Real, noting a hotel on the opposite side going in the direction of the drovers'. He freed his horse and took it round the back of the hotel, to re-tether it to a rail there.

He had decided not to do the thing in the open street. He knew the sheriff would keep out of it — there was no problem there — but if the deed was carried out too blatantly, some bystanders might get a good description of the perpetrator and pass it on to authorities out of town.

Alongside the hotel there were steps giving access to the roof. He drew his rifle from its scabbard. He bent down and took a handful of dirt, then rubbed it along the length of the barrel to reduce its sheen.

He mounted the steps slowly, careful not to make too much noise. On the top he walked up and down behind the low false-front till he found a comfortable vantage point. He shifted the poncho to give him clearance, jacked a round into his rifle and settled down in wait. He was in no rush. His victim had a meal to finish. I hope the bozo enjoys it, he mused to himself, as it's his last. Roscoe Styles did have some compassion.

After some twenty minutes, he saw Johnny emerge from the adobe feeding-parlour. Feeling excitement rising in him, Roscoe pinched out the half-finished cigarette. He watched as Johnny settled his hat back on his head. As he hoped, the man started walking back to the drovers'. Roscoe put his cheek against the rifle stock and took aim.

The rifle moved in a practised grip,

tracking his quarry along the board-walk. Easy as a turkey-shoot, he mused.

As the man drew level with the hotel, Roscoe's finger tightened on the trigger.

Suddenly two shots cracked almost simultaneously, their echoes slamming back and forth between the buildings along the street.

Johnny dived to the boards as the shop window behind him shattered, rolling till he fell to dirt level with the sidewalk planking giving part cover.

From his prone position he looked around. On a roof on the other side of the street a figure was staggering. A rifle dropped from the man's hand and the fellow spent seconds trying clumsily to grab at something for support. But his uncoordinated fingers failed to make a purchase and, in front of wide-eyed townsfolk on the Calle Real, he pitched forward, his poncho billowing like the wings of some giant bat. In his downward trajectory he hit an awning, bouncing off to thump noisily into the dirt of the street.

Johnny got to his feet to see a figure, levering out a spent load from a rifle, emerge from an alley a block to his left. The man reloaded and levelled the gun in one quick movement as, on Johnny's right, another gunman stepped into the sunlight. The first slowly crossed to the fallen body while the second mounted the boardwalk and approached Johnny, crunching glass shards underfoot. 'You OK, pal?'

'What the blue hell's going on?'

'Just saved your skin, that's what.'

The man bent down and pulled back the poncho that was now covering the bushwhacker's face. 'Roscoe Styles.'

'What the frig has it got to do with you?'

'For a start I'm the guy who just punched your lights out.'

'Son of a . . . ' The downed man's voice trailed away.

The rifleman considered the blood-ied, twisted frame. 'I'll tell you one thing, Roscoe. You must have the constitution of a hoss. What you've just

been through, you should be dead now.'
He threw a glance at the crowd now
hesitantly edging forward. 'Will one of
you folk fetch the doc?'

He looked back at the fallen man,
noted the spreading redness on his
shirt-front. He took off the man's
bandanna and wedged it between the
cloth and the wound.

'What the hell you muscle in for?'
Styles wheezed when he'd finished.
'You gotta be law and I was told the law
would keep its nose out of things.'

'We're territorial agents. Not local
law.'

'Prescott men? I ain't no concern of
the Territory. I ain't crossed no county
lines.'

The man shrugged. 'We got our
business to do.'

The other lawman watched as the
fallen man coughed blood. 'We're more
interested in Manzoni than you.'

The man moved his head weakly.
'Manzoni, the bastard,' he spluttered.
'He said it was a straight job.'

At that juncture, a neat-suited man joined them. 'I'm a doctor.'

'He's all yours, Doc.'

Johnny looked from one lawman to the other. 'What's this all about?'

'There someplace we can talk?' the one with the rifle asked.

'Only place I got title to is a drover's pallet. But don't see that as the place for a quiet parley if that's what you mean.'

The man gestured to some empty chairs on the boardwalk. 'That'll do.' They crossed over and sat down.

One leant across to Johnny. 'You heard the talk out there, we're territorial officers. Well, I'm Marshal Shaw and this is Deputy Kane.'

Johnny nodded.

'What you want to kill Manzoni for?' Shaw went on.

Johnny was no stranger to putting on a dumb show for badge carriers. 'Me? Kill somebody? No, you got me wrong, sir. I don't want to kill nobody.'

'You're a long way from home,

pilgrim. What you doing out here in the Territory?'

'Visiting friends.'

Shaw shook his head. 'It's going to be easier for you if you open up, kid.' He was about to continue when a young lad in short knickerbockers interrupted. 'Doc says to come over to his place quick, mister.'

'Don't run away,' Shaw said to Johnny, adding: 'Keep an eye on him,' to his colleague.

In the surgery the failed assassin was fast failing himself. 'Doc says I ain't got long. I been shot up enough times in my life to figure he's right on that. Now it's a cert I'm going, point is, I want a good funeral. Manzoni was paying me a grand for this caper. Five hundred when I done the job and . . . ' He tried to indicate his jacket pocket. 'And five hundred in there. That should cover a big do, shouldn't it?'

'Six black horses, whatever you want.'

'Only thing that sticks in my craw is

that Manzoni didn't tell me what a mess this was when he hired me. Easy job, in and out, he said. The jerk-off didn't say nothing about Prescott agents. Him and his fine suits and fine ways. You gonna nail him?'

'Got nothing on him. Not even this. We got no proof it was on his orders. Just our word against his. Anyways, like you say, it's a local matter.'

The man's lids fell. 'Well, I'll tell you something for free,' he croaked without opening his eyes. 'You want to nail him, he ain't here in Tucson. He's hiding out with a couple of his sidekicks in a cabin up in the hills. He's got a flash hunting-lodge up there. Nobody knows he's up there 'cept me. I was supposed to ride up there when I'd finished the job; let him know when it was all clear and get the rest of my money.'

'Where's the cabin?'

'Up in the Rincon foothills.' Slowly, further directions were given in a fading voice. Eventually nothing.

'Our poncho friend didn't make it,'

Shaw said, back on the sidewalk. He informed his colleague what he had learned. 'Awkward critter didn't get the whole location out before he snuffed — but I heard enough to know where it is.'

He took a map from his pocket and began studying it. He threw a glance at his colleague. 'Put him in the picture,' he instructed and returned to his map.

'See it's this way,' Kane began. 'We got aspirations to see Arizona get statehood. And it's the way of things that we have to prove to Washington that we deserve it. But there's several things standing in the way. For example, we have to prove we have established law and order; and can maintain it. With crooks like Manzoni high in the roost that's kind of difficult. Worse, with his contacts and pull he'll be in top running for the governorship and there's no way we want his kind in that position.'

'Well, if he's such a crook, how come the authorities don't charge him and get him into court.'

The officer grunted. 'Easier said than done. For a start, like I said, as a big businessman and local politician he's already a big wheel, well in with the authorities. Second, he's been such a wily critter that we don't have anything that would stand up in court. Leastways, not against a good defence lawyer — and he could afford the best.'

'I still don't see why you're telling me all this.'

Kane took out a pack of factory-made cigarettes and offered one. After he'd lit the two cigarettes he continued. 'That's what you and we have in common. We know he's an all-out lawbreaking varmint. We got stuff on him but, like you, nothing that will stand up in a court of law.'

'You still haven't explained — what's this got to do with me?' Johnny didn't trust crushers. He'd never co-operated with them and he didn't intend to start now.

Shaw put down the map and joined

them, histrionically wafting the cigarette smoke away with his hand, and took up the conversation. 'Let's say somebody comes out here, I don't know, say a stranger from back East. Now if he were to put our mutual friend Manzoni under the dirt we would deem that a favour. In return we would see to it that this fellow could leave the territory unimpeded. Safe passage over the territorial line. No matter what he'd done here — or anywhere else.'

Johnny began to wonder what they knew. 'Still don't know what you're talking about.'

The marshal ignored the pretence of innocence and continued. 'Only snag is, Manzoni is a bit of a yellow-back. Got all worried about some maverick wanting to put his lights out so he's aiming to hole up a spell. Now this fellow who wants to nail him — this hypothetical fellow we're talking about — would need to know where.'

Johnny pulled a wry face and

nodded. 'I suppose he would.'

The marshal showed Johnny the map and where he had pencilled a small circle. 'Well, it's there. I've just learnt that from the feller who took a potshot at you.'

He explained in detail how to get to it.

'Can I have the map?' Johnny asked.

Marshal Shaw smiled. 'That's my boy. Now you're going to have to be careful. He's got two gunnies around him. Maybe three. We'll stay out of the way. We have to, we gotta keep our hands clean. That means you'll have to handle it all by yourself.' He smiled. 'But from what I hear that might not be the problem it seems on the face of it.'

Johnny studied the map, traced his finger between Tucson and the cabin location. Then he shrugged. 'Anything else I should know?'

'No, that's about it,' Shaw said, sticking out his hand. 'Luck, feller.'

Johnny pushed the map into one of the deep pockets of his long slicker. 'Be seeing you fellows.'

They watched him walk down the boardwalk towards the turn-off to the drovers'.

'Poor bastard,' Kane said when he was out of earshot. 'Don't rate his chances much. Why did you set him up like that?'

'I'm clutching at straws. There's an outside chance he could pull it off. From what we know of him he's mean enough.'

'More likely he'll get hisself killed.'

'Yeah, but we ain't gonna be *too* far away. We'll see what happens. And if he does get blasted that could finally give us something concrete to pin on Manzoni. Either way we win.'

12

The first thing he noticed was the thin tendril of smoke. Closer he could see the chimney from which it emanated. Eventually he could make out the whole cabin. He took his time studying the place. It was a neat, well-built thing, not as rough as others he had seen on his journey out. Built to the specification of a rich man, an oasis of luxury in a wilderness. Most important, it stood alone in a space with no adjacent buildings. It was designed as a hunting-lodge, not a fortification to be defended.

Only snag was the single approach to it was an open stretch of sandstone. Limited cover was provided by some pine to the side, near to the cabin.

The types of men they were, they would be on guard. But he had an advantage. They would not be expecting *him*. So they would not be fully alert and there would be no traps.

And the poncho he had claimed from the dead Roscoe should fool them for a while.

He was weary from the travel. But in his game, tiredness came with the territory and he still retained the alertness and capability for action that had seen him through countless scrapes on the East Side.

He came to rest some hundred yards from the cabin. In case he had already been seen and even now was being carefully watched, he didn't linger. He pulled the hat low over his eyes, swung down from the horse and began a slow advance. 'Hallo, the cabin,' he shouted after some paces. Faces appeared at the window. Covered the way he was, he would be too far away for them to see details. 'Roscoe Styles,' he shouted, continuing his advance.

He made his gait as casual as possible. Further on he shouted, 'The bastard's dead.'

'Is that really you, Roscoe?' someone shouted.

'Cut the shit,' Johnny shouted back. 'I've come for the rest of my money.'

'How much would that be?'

'Five hundred owing.'

That must have been the clincher because two men appeared at the door. Nevertheless they held rifles. They separated and moved forward on the veranda. He couldn't leave it too long. The closer he got the chancier it became. It wouldn't be long before they saw something was wrong.

He continued his slow advance, a rage burning within him that defied thoughts of safety.

There was little Johnny didn't know about guns and their use. Left hand, right hand. And firing rifles from the hip, although not a position to be favoured, did not present the problem to him that it would to other bearers of arms. And he had a cocked rifle in each hand. A split second before use he pushed the barrels down so that their

174

ends appeared below the poncho — enabling the garment to be clear when he raised the guns to firing position.

Then he shifted to the side and up they came, spitting fire.

One man was knocked sprawling backwards to slump against the wall. The defenceless and awkward position in which he landed indicated it was all over for him.

Johnny dropped the other with a bullet that appeared to strike the man in the hip in such a way that he fell to the boards with a cry of anguish.

Shots crackled from the cabin as Johnny made a dash for the cover of the pine at the side. Before he reached it a shot burned across his arm. It came from the remaining fellow on the veranda who still held his pistol and was using it to fire from his prone position. The critter was a sitting duck but, still in the open, so was Johnny and he instinctively returned fire while running. Once in the trees he could see that his shot had put paid to the man.

Now, if Manzoni had three sidekicks, that meant there were only two men left inside, Manzoni himself and a remaining heavy. He discarded the clumsy poncho and opened his long buckskin jacket to peer down the sleeve and check his arm. There was blood and it was smarting, but he had other things to think about.

He appraised his situation. He was in an alien environment. He didn't know the ways of the West and he was a beginner at the horse-riding business. He was unfamiliar with the damn climate, the terrains were strange to him, and he didn't know about rattlesnakes and such. But one thing he did know: he was a competent fighting man.

He contemplated the cabin, which had now gone quiet. There were two men left. He imagined what was going on in there. Manzoni, who had always used others for his dirty work, would now feel like a rat in a tightening trap.

His sidekick knew that all his hardcase buddies had been wiped out; he was the only one of the bunch left.

Right, time for some stretching of nerves.

He snuggled the rifle against his shoulder and took careful aim. He fired and a window smashed in. Slowly he took another sighting and shattered a second. Then a third window went. There would be glass all over the place in there. And unexpected, jarring shots. Confusion was his object.

And it worked. Through the open doorway he heard a raised voice.

'Don't care what you say, Manzoni. He might be an Easterner but he sure ain't no tenderfoot.'

He could just make out a voice further in: 'Hell, he's just one man, Piker.'

'One man? He's a goddamn one-man army. With those two out there he's killed *six* of our best men. For all we know he's downed Roscoe. I'm telling you, he ain't human.'

Then a figure with raised arms came to the doorway. 'Hold your fire, mister. I'm coming out.'

Didn't look like a bluff, but Johnny kept his rifle ready.

The man stepped gingerly forward. But at the top step there came a crack from the interior and he pitched forward.

All was still.

And all was silent, save for the drone of insects in the heat and the lone caw of some bird flying overhead.

A bluff? Johnny studied the fallen figure. The man had gone down too heavily to look faked. And he wasn't armed.

Johnny worked his way through the trees, watching the cabin but still keeping half an eye on the fallen man. Eventually he got to such an elevation he could see the back of the fellow. Sure enough, there was a stain on his back. It wasn't a ruse.

Finding a good vantage point that provided cover, he lay down and put a shot through the darkness of the doorway. Then he remained still and quiet for a long time, with the intention of adding to the war of nerves.

After a spell he shouted, 'You're all alone now, Manzoni. It's just you and me.'

He lit a smoke, getting satisfaction from teasing the man, then shouted, 'You can't sit there for ever. If you make a break for it — you're a dead man. Better just walk out with your hands up.'

When the cigarette was burned down he stubbed it in the dirt and called, 'No use waiting for nightfall. I got some turpentine here.' He laughed. 'Come nightfall I'm gonna *burn* you out.'

That was a bluff but he reckoned Manzoni wouldn't put it to the test.

'Who are you?' came the shout after a while.

Johnny continued with his game of making the man sweat.

'The Expediter,' he boomed as sonorously as possible. All part of the confusion.

'What's it all about?' Manzoni shouted. 'What do you want?'

'You come outside and we can talk face to face. Clear the air.'

'You'll just gun me down like you done everybody else.'

'Tell you what, I'll back off out of range and we can talk that way.'

There followed a long-drawn out silence. Then: 'OK. But you step out first.'

'As you wish,' Johnny retorted and began working his way back through the trees to give himself some distance. Still wary of possible trickery he kept vigilance on the cabin. Then he dropped down to the sandstone and into the open. 'That OK?' he yelled, making a show of backing some paces.

Manzoni emerged from the darkness of the doorway. He wore side-pistols but had no rifle.

'Come clear of the cabin so I can see you,' Johnny shouted, stepping further back in encouragement.

Some ten yards away from the cabin,

Manzoni yelled, 'Now are you going to tell me what's this all about?'

'My brother, Brendan Doyle. You had him killed.'

Manzoni shook his head. 'Don't know the name.'

'I guess you don't at that. All the operations you got going, a name here and there ain't gonna mean much. The guy, my brother, he had red hair, like me.'

'You ain't got red hair.'

Johnny began to move forward, walking an unflinching course, straight up the centre of the sandstone. 'I did have. And a red beard.'

'So you — the man who calls himself the Expediter — and that Easterner who came to Sangrano some time back — you're the same man?'

'On the button.'

Manzoni chewed on it, then shouted, 'Anyways, however your brother died, it was nothing to do with me.'

'I'm here to settle scores, not to argue.'

'How?'

Johnny came to a standstill. '*Mano a mano*, as they say out here,' he shouted. 'Just you and me, face to face.'

'Ain't just,' Manzoni mouthed. 'My hand-pistols are no good at that range. Even as an Easterner, you should know that. You could drop me easy as a coon with that Winchester.'

'True,' Johnny said, moving forward a few paces.

'No, that ain't much better.'

Keeping the rifle levelled from the hip, Johnny studied his adversary. 'OK — *mano a mano* — with fists. If you think that would make it more equal. In fact, punching that ugly mug of yours might give me greater satisfaction. So the deal is — I beat you, I take you in. Right?'

Manzoni thought about it. 'I'd go along with that.'

Johnny nodded. He dropped the rifle and resumed his walk towards the object of his hatred.

Manzoni began to walk towards him

and felt a satisfactory anticipation surge up inside. He noted Johnny's hands hanging loosely at his sides. The buckskin jacket was open and whipping loosely back in the breeze that was now cutting across the open sandstone — and there was no gunbelt, no holsters. No gun stuck in his trouser belt. The man was unarmed and a fool. A greenhorn Easterner used to the niceties of city life with its established law, not realizing that out here there were no rules. With the nearest lawman twenty miles away, there would be no comeback for gunning down an unarmed man. All he had to do was wait until he was in range, up close.

'Come on then, city boy,' he goaded, rubbing his knuckles in pretence of preparing for a fist fight, and trying to stifle any appearance of the triumph surging up inside.

The arrogant stranger continued his casual advance until, some twenty feet away, he suddenly stopped.

Manzoni halted after a few more

paces. Suddenly *he* was enjoying the game. 'Come on,' he urged, putting forward his balled fists, unconcerned that the stranger didn't look as though he was yet prepared for a scrap, his hands still hanging loose, slightly back of his waist.

'What's the matter?' Manzoni challenged. 'Having second thoughts?'

For some reason the stranger remained immobile, unperturbed by the gang boss's gibing. Manzoni pondered on the situation. Why had the guy stopped? Twenty feet was too much elbowroom for a fist-fight. Must be scared.

He'd intended waiting until the stranger was up real close before blasting the life out of the critter. But now there was an unexpected delay. Oh, what the hell? — twenty feet put the man well within killing range of his hand-guns. Even though he was not the best of shots, emptying two guns in the man's direction — he was bound to hit him. His lips stirred with the hint of a smile.

He waited for one more second before making his play. But even before his hand had reached his gunhandle, the stranger had pitched forward to the ground — as though he had been well prepared for Manzoni's treachery.

Consternation flashed across the older man's face as he agitatedly fanned and fired. But slugs whistled ineffectively overhead or gouted up chunks of sandstone, his aim being thrown by the surprise of his adversary's sudden action; along with the fact that lying prone had reduced the man's size as a target.

The look of consternation on his face became one of bewilderment as a gun appeared from nowhere in the stranger's hand. Then, just one explosion from the levelled cannon was enough to remove any further expression from Manzoni's visage. In fact there was no sign of anything on his face other than the crater in his forehead. Death spasms worked his trigger finger as he caromed backwards, harmlessly cleaving the air above with his remaining shots.

Johnny stood up. After checking there was to be no further gunplay, he slipped the huge Beaumont-Adams through the slit he'd cut in the side of his jacket and returned it to the specially designed harness across his back. In the small of his back so that only an astute frisker would find it.

The harness that he had had bespoke-made by a Jewish leather-worker in the Bronx many years ago, tailor-fitted to his body to reduce its awkwardness. A contrivance that had seen him through more gun battles than he could tally.

He knocked dust from his clothes as he casually walked over to the corpse to confirm for himself the finality of the proceedings.

Epilogue

He sat in the saddle, content to follow the walking motion of the horse. Birds were chirping in the thickets as he wended his way along the track towards the Blanchard place. Sighting the girl he returned her wave with his good arm. The wound in his other had been bandaged but it insisted on reminding him of its existence with the occasional twinge.

'I've dropped in to return a horse,' he said, as she skipped towards him, 'and to thank you for your kindnesses.'

'Is it all over?'

'It's all over.'

He dismounted and recounted the recent events.

'It must have been horrendous,' she said when he'd rounded off the tale.

'It's been a nasty, dirty business all right, but ain't been as worrying as it might sound. It's the kind of business I know.'

She looked puzzled but at that juncture Mr Blanchard appeared, having completed some chore in the barn.

'Sure seeing you a lot around the place, young feller,' he said. 'Are you my little girl's new beau?' He was at the age when the forthrightness of infancy was now reasserting itself over the everyday politeness of the long-past intervening years.

Mary closed her eyes and shook her head at the lack of diplomacy.

Johnny smiled and glanced at her. 'No, sir, but I sure envy the man who is.'

'Pity,' her father said, and continued into the building, leaving the young people to their conversation.

'You're leaving now, aren't you?' she prompted, her voice falling. 'I can tell.'

He nodded.

'I was hoping you'd stay.'

He turned and looked at the horizon. 'This wild country speaks a language other than mine. It's big and empty.

Fact is, it's hard to see that it's on the same planet that holds Fifth Avenue.' He looked back at her. 'But there's part of me going to hate leaving.'

'Do you really have to go?'

'I've got a life elsewhere . . . one I haven't told you about.'

She studied his eyes as he spoke. 'All this shooting and killing, it hasn't affected you as it might any other man I know.' Then, after further contemplation: 'This life of yours in New York — yes, I think I'm beginning to understand.'

He nodded. 'I have to confess, Mary, it's been a long time since I been on the side of decency.'

'Will things change when you return home?'

'We're bound by our past.'

Moisture welled up in her eyes and she gave a little murmuring sound. 'Hold me.'

She felt good in his arms. There was a goodness in the moment that transcended the bleakness of his life ahead — the only life he knew. And he was embarrassed at his appetite for the woman, knowing that, as things stood, it was not to be. If only, if only . . .

'Well that's that, Johnny Doyle.' She kissed his cheek and pulled away. 'Will I ever see you again?'

He held her at arm's length, looked into her eyes. 'We don't know what life holds.'

'Well, if ever life's wheel spins you out this way again, you'll come by and see me? I'll still be here.'

He raised her hand and kissed it. 'You can bet on it.'

For a few moments their eyes continued the embrace then she said, 'Come. I'll get the rig and drive you into town.'

★ ★ ★

Marshal Shaw entered the Territorial Police office in Prescott with the meditative air of a man who had had a rough night. His chief had wanted a report on the killings in the south-west of the territory. Because of the scale of events the report had been required fast and it had been midnight before he had completed it, concluding that the mass slaughtering was the result of warfare between border gangs.

Deputy Kane was sitting in his boss's chair, his feet in the trash-basket like he owned the place. At the sight of his chief he leapt to his feet, stubbed out his cigarette on the floor and stood to attention, exclaiming, 'Sir!'

The marshal ignored the salute and dropped into his chair. For a moment he studied the burns along the edges of his desk. 'Jeez, I can't understand how these burns get here — when I don't even smoke. You know what? I . . . ' Shrugging, he left the sentence incomplete. 'So, what's new?'

Kane pointed to a piece of paper on the desk. 'Wire in from New York, sir. A 'search and find' on one of their gangmen out there. Name of Johnny Doyle. Wanted for murder. Crossed state lines. Last known to be heading for Sangrano, Arizona.'

The marshal read the missive and looked at his subordinate.

'See what it says?' Kane prompted. 'Red-haired. Just shy of medium height. Irish stock. Brother of Brendan Doyle. You know, the guy in Sangrano cemetery.'

The marshal nodded. Then: 'But this Johnny Doyle . . . rings no bells with me. What about you?'

'But ain't he — ?'

'Like I said, rings no bells with me? And you?'

Kane paused. 'Never heard of him, boss.'

Marshal Shaw screwed up the paper and tossed it into the basket. 'You know what, Kane? I got a feeling someday you might make a good officer.'

★   ★   ★

With a raucous 'Giddap!' the driver flicked the ribbons and the stage began to roll. Soon it was doing a fair lick out of Sangrano on the eastbound route.

Aboard was Johnny, once again attired in his Eastern clothes and derby.

'Jesus,' he grunted to himself as the vehicle rose up the grade. 'How do we stop this thing?' he wanted to know of his fellow passengers.

'Stop?' one asked.

He looked vainly at their questioning faces but he hadn't got time for a lengthy debate. He stood up and banged on the roof. With metal rims rasping on the gravel of the grade neither driver or shotgun could hear his rappings, muffled even more by the baggage stacked topside.

He opened the door and, grabbing the roof-rail, he heaved himself up and clambered onto the top.

'Could you stop at the cemetery?' he yelled through the racket. 'Just for a brief spell. I'd be obliged.'

The driver threw a surprised glance back at his acrobatic passenger. 'The cemetery?' He hauled on the ribbons.

'OK, but make it short.'

By the time the stage had creaked to a standstill they were some fifty yards past the plot. Johnny dropped down. He walked back along the trail gathering orange Mexican poppies from the flora that decorated the side of the track.

By the time he was nearing the cemetery he had collected a large bunch.

'There you are, you big lunk,' he said a minute later, laying them on his brother's grave. 'Don't say I never do anything for you.'

He didn't linger, simply made the sign of the cross out of instinct and headed back.

'OK, Mr Coachman,' he said on his return. 'Thank you for your forbearance. You can get your conveyance under way again.'

Soon the cemetery was far behind them, just a faint tinge of orange still discernible on one of the graves.

It had suddenly come to him that

he'd had instructions to lay flowers on his brother's grave. That had been the whole point in coming out here.

Johnny Doyle could lie to anybody.

But not to his mother.

Other titles in the
Linford Western Library:

HONDO COUNTY GUNDOWN

Chad Hammer

The Valley of the Wolf was no place for strangers, but Chet Beautel was not the usual breed of drifter. He was a straight-shooting man of the mountains searching for something better than what lay behind. Instead, he encountered a new brand of terror enshrouded in a mystery which held a thousand people hostage — until he saddled up to challenge it with a mountain man's grit and courage, backed up by a blazing .45. If Wolf Valley was ever to be peaceful again, Chet Beautel would be that peacemaker.

RETURN TO RIO DIABLO

Wade Vanmarten

After killing the drug-crazed son of a powerful man, Deputy Sheriff Brimmer Stone is forced to resign his post and leave Houston. He and his best friend return to Rio Diablo, a wide-open Texas town that holds memories of youthful adventure and romance for them both. There, Stone rekindles a love affair, while his friend makes plans to take his new love away from the fancy house where she works and marry her. The sudden and brutal murder of his friend sends Stone on a quest for revenge that sets off a bloody war . . .

TRAIL OF THE REAPER

B. J. Holmes

Bounty-hunter Jonathan Grimm — the man they called the Reaper — took a break from his man-hunting to attend a family wedding. But a shooting on the doorstep hurled him back into his man-chasing role. Then, what started out as a straightforward chase ran him smack into hard-case gunmen aiming to cut him down. At the tail end of his life, how could he afford to keep tangling with younger, trigger-happy gunnies? But one thing was a dead cert — before the last man was left standing, a lot of lead was going to fly.

GREENWOOD VENDETTA

Frank Fields

Billy Nesbitt is released from prison after serving thirty years for a crime he did not commit, and he sets out to exact retribution from the man really responsible. However, his target, James Fairfax, a landowner in Greenwood, is expecting Billy and tries to prevent him ever reaching the town. Billy's quest becomes a battle between his desire for revenge and his conscience. He has some difficult choices to make and questions to answer — but can he survive long enough to see justice done?